Hooligan Agor

To Carol with an

©**Gussy Gassam 2022**

INTRODUCTION

This is yet another book on Wakefield's notorious hard man, Paul Sykes, but with one notable difference. It is a collection of stories about how Mr Sykes, or Sykesy as he was known to his friends, became the leader of Yorkshire's most infamous football hooligan firm, the Leeds United Service Crew, while still in his teens … and the violence that followed.

It is a story of bloodshed, drunkenness, and the many street brawls that plagued the man throughout this turbulent period in his life.

It was Thomas Hardy who said, *"Though a good deal is too strange to be believed, nothing is too strange to have happened,"* and when you read this book you may well conclude that many of the stories regarding Sykesy's days as one of Britain's most notorious football hooligans listed here, may be too strange to be believed. However, none were too strange to have happened, as hooligans up and down the country have testified during the compiling of this book.

Gussy Gassam
Wakefield
November 2020

BARRY GATES

I was leader of Leeds United Service Crew back in 1962, when football hooliganism was not as revered as it is today ... and no one had even dreamed of writing a book about their hooligan activities.

I first came across Paul Sykes when I heard he had knocked out one of our firm when the latter had been visiting his girlfriend over in Wakefield. In fact, Sykes had not only knocked him out but given him such a beating the poor lad had ended up sampling hospital food for a month. I was incensed that anybody could do that to one of our mob, so I got the lads together and we drove over to Wakefield to teach the little bastard that the Leeds United Service Crew were not a mob to piss about with.

We travelled down in a convoy of cars and when we got there, we asked for directions to the Lupset Estate where we knew Sykes lived. We knew that because the girlfriend of the lad he had beaten up had told us. Once we had driven to his house, we pulled up outside it before going over and knocking on his door.

He wasn't in, but his dad was. I quickly explained the purpose of our visit and added we would be in the Buck and Vine pub near Elland Road on Saturday at midday if he wanted to come over and explain himself. We then took our leave, but not before I added, with a touch of malice, that it would be better if he did come up to Leeds to see us, because it would save us the bother of having to come to Wakefield to look for him again.

Come Saturday we were sitting in the Buck and Vine waiting for our spotters to locate the Crystal Palace firm so we could go and have a ruck with them, when the lad we had posted outside the pub to stop the Palace mob sneaking up on us, came flying through the door before crashing to the deck and out for the count.

He had clearly been punched and my immediate reaction was that the Crystal Palace mob had arrived and had taken him by surprise, which is why he had not rushed in to tell us our opponents were there as he usually did on these occasions. Still, we all jumped up expecting a bunch of lads to rush through the door and attack us but none did. Instead, this tall lad with dark hair and bulging biceps calmly walked in before looking around.

Staying as cool as a cucumber, he said, "Good afternoon, gentlemen. My name is Paul Sykes and I understand you have been looking for me."

We were gobsmacked, and stared at him in surprise. Although we had told his father it would be better for him if he came to our local to explain himself, we never, in our wildest dreams, expected him to do so – or if he did, that he would come alone and not mob-handed. So, we just stared at him as though he was some kind of simpleton who had escaped from the local nuthouse. But, before we could do anything more there was a lot of yelling and screaming outside and a bottle came crashing through the window missing my head by inches.

I was furious and thinking Sykes had come to the pub mob-handed after all, I moved towards him angrily, with my fists clenched. He however, was glaring out of the window looking as surprised as I was. When I looked out I saw a tough looking mob wearing Crystal Palace scarves and I realised that their mob had arrived and that they had nothing to do with Sykes. His next words confirmed it.

"Who the fuck are this lot?" he asked, fixing me with a scowl. "Friends of yours?"

I shook my head. "No the Crystal Palace mob."

"The Crystal Palace mob?"

I nodded. "Yeah football hooligans from London who have come to fight us."

"Fight you..."

"Yea, we're the Leeds United Service Crew, and we follow Leeds United up and down the country to fight fellow hooligans. Has nobody ever told you?"

He shook his head. "Never heard of you mate."

I was fuming, but before I could say anything else he went outside and beckoned the lads and me to follow him.

Once outside the pub, the Crystal Palace firm stopped yelling and their leader stepped forward and said, "I'm Chubby Hancock, Palace's top boy. Who's your top boy?"

"I am," said Sykes, before I could speak. "I'm their top boy."

I gave him a look, but before I could say anything he moved towards Hancock and asked him what he wanted.

"I want a fight with you," replied Hancock. "What the fuck do you think I want? One top boy versus another."

Sykes smiled and headbutted him so hard he crashed to the ground, clearly unconscious. His mates were shocked and began to back away nervously, but Sykes moved towards them and belted one in the face followed by another and then another and another, sending all three crashing to the ground.

    I was gobsmacked and at first I just stood there looking on in awe because I had never seen anything like it in my life. I quickly pulled myself together and told the rest of the lads to help Sykes, but the Palace firm were already in disarray. When they saw us rushing towards them, they did a runner leaving us to chase after them and Sykes to finish punching the hell out of the lad he had started attacking.

DAZ FORMBY

I too was a member of Leeds United Service Crew back in 1962 and I remember the incident Barry Gates talks about in the first chapter very well ... and with good reason. I was the guy standing outside the pub keeping an eye out for the Crystal Palace mob. Sykes had appeared out of nowhere and punched me full on in the face, sending me crashing through the door and leaving me flat out on the ground.

To be honest, I felt like I had been hit by a double-decker bus when I came to my senses and thought the bastard responsible would be long gone. So, I was somewhat staggered to discover him laughing and chatting with Gates and the rest of the lads as though they were old friends and what he had done to me was of no consequence.

I was even more staggered when I was told that this was the infamous Paul Sykes who I had been hearing so much about of late. My first instinct was to go over and punch the bastard in the face for assaulting me, but I was also intrigued as to why he and the lads were suddenly so pally. When I was told that he had knocked out Palace's top boy without breaking into a sweat, I was glad I had not hit him because God knows what would have happened if I had.

I mean Sykes was the hardest bastard I have ever known. He was a bruiser through and through and loved a good punch up whenever the opportunity arose, which is why he aligned himself with the Leeds Service Crew. I don't think he was ever interested in football itself, most hooligans aren't. Most hooligans don't go to football grounds to support their team, but to take part in a punch up with rival hooligans. In that respect, Paul Sykes and I had something in common.

Another thing we had in common is that we were not bullies. We didn't go around hitting people for no reason just to show how hard we were, as that overgrown vegetable Lee Duffy would do when he was top boy of Middlesbrough's hooligan firm, the Frontline in the eighties. I say overgrown vegetable because that is how Sykes always referred to Duffy when talking about him in public or in private.

I can remember one time when I was visiting Sykesy in prison and he told me Duffy was there too, but the authorities had decided to separate them. Sykesy had challenged him to a fight, but Duffy had burst out in tears at the very thought of fighting him and asked to be put in isolation for his own protection.

That was the eighties though, when Sykes was no longer active with the Leeds Service Crew and not 1962 when he first joined the firm. Back then, Duffy hadn't even been born and Sykesy's biggest rival was anybody who fancied his chances against him and came at him with all guns blazing. Normally, these people were hooligans who came at him mob-handed, because that is what hooligans do, attack each other in packs, and I must say I saw him engage in some scraps with them when they did.

I can remember one occasion when we got Aldershot away and there were about fifty of them and twenty of us, but that did not stop Sykesy steaming into them with everything he had and knocking them out one after another. He was fascinating to watch and indeed I once got knocked out because of it. I had been watching him steam into a couple of

Northampton hooligans, when out of the blue I was struck from behind and wound up in a pool of blood. I did actually black out but not before I saw Sykes rush up and headbutt the bastard responsible ... making sure he saw stars too.

But what was really fascinating about Sykes was that he loved challenging top boys to a fight. You would think that top boys were always challenging each other to a fight wouldn't you, to show they were harder than their rivals were ... but they didn't. For that you have Charlie McFudden to thank.

This is because back in the fifties, McFudden was the leader of Blackburn's hooligan firm, the Mill Hill Mob and he took football violence to a whole new level by chopping off the head of Burnley's top boy Damon Kerr and sticking it on the gates of Burnley's ground, Turf Moor, for all to see. He did the same with other Burnley hooligans after they had humiliated him in front of his firm, earning the nickname Chainsaw Charlie in the process. Since then, many top boys had been wary of challenging other top boys to a fight, in case, like Burnley's top boy, they wound up getting their heads chopped off because of another psychopath lurking amongst them.

Still, not all top boys were afraid to challenge other top boys to a fight, as Crystal Palace top boy Chubby Hancock had shown when he had turned up outside our local boozer and done precisely that in the previous chapter. In fact he loved it and so did Sykes.

I can remember one time when Mad Mike Mongrel came to Leeds, and demanded Sykes have a one to one with him to prove he was the harder of the two. Mongrel was the leader of Stoke's firm the Naughty Forty and a raving lunatic, but Sykes just laughed at him before punching him so hard in the face he spent the next week in intensive care being fed via a drip.

But the fight I remember the most was against Derby County hard man Benny Morgan. Morgan was not only their top boy but also a hardened criminal, having served time in prison for various offences including wounding with intent. I had my doubts Sykes would win against Morgan. This was because Morgan was a mountain of a man, standing seven feet tall, and it was like David fighting Goliath, even though Sykes himself was six foot three and not small himself.

Morgan took the first swing at Sykes which he easily dodged before Sykes moved forward and hit Morgan with a flurry of punches to the head, body, and face. It was good stuff and many a man would have buckled, but Morgan was protected by layers of flab and so the blows to his body did not do as much damage as otherwise they

might. Neither, did the blows to his head, because with Morgan being a good seven inches taller than Sykes, most of them did not connect properly ... or if they did, it wasn't with the full power of his punch behind them because of Morgan's vast height.

Sykes continued to pound at Morgan's ribs and stomach hoping to double him up so he could smack him in the face and hopefully knock him out. Although he did get a lot of good punches into Morgan's face, it still wasn't enough, particularly as he managed to get in a few good punches of his own and on one occasion sent Sykes crashing to the floor.

I thought it was over, and so did everybody else watching the fight. But it soon became apparent it wasn't, because to everybody's surprise Sykes sat up and went to get to his feet looking very pissed off as he did. Morgan moved forward to kick him in the head, but it was a mistake because Sykes somehow caught his foot and brought Morgan crashing to the ground, banging his head in the process. I thought he was out for the count but he wasn't, so Sykes began jumping up and down on his head before kicking him ferociously in the face. This time Morgan really was out and Sykes was the winner.

As I said before, Sykes was the hardest bastard I have ever known or am likely to know. He's dead now, God rest his soul. But that's how I knew him and that's how I will remember him. RIP Paul Sykes.

LUKE THOMPSON

I was a member of the Leeds Service Crew in 1962 and was the guy that Sykes had beaten up and put in intensive care. This was what had led to Barry Gates going down to confront him at his house along with the rest of the lads.

It occurred as a consequence of a chance meeting I had with him in early 1962 when I was dating a girl over in Wakefield by the name of Joanne Bickerstaff. What happened was we were on our way to the pictures to watch The Day of The Triffids, a film I had been dying to see for quite some considerable time, when Joanne suggested we stop off at a pub to get a drink. I was surprised because we had already agreed to get to the pictures early, because lots of people wanted to see the film and we couldn't be sure of getting tickets if we got there later.

So, we went inside the pub and once we had got the drinks she asked about my football hooligan activities and which firm the Leeds Service Crew and I would be fighting this week.

I wasn't surprised by the question because all girls like naughty boys and let's face it all hooligans are naughty boys. We have to be, given we spend our time fighting and punching the hell out of our rivals. So I told her that we would be up against the Hull City Psychos. I said the last time our firms had met they had legged it, but only after we had kicked the fuck out of them with me headbutting one guy, and punching another to the ground, before kicking him in the head and laying him out cold.

Bickerstaff was impressed as girls often are with tough guys and started clapping and saying what a tough guy I was. In fact she said, "You're the toughest guy around," which was good for my ego, and brought a huge smile to my face.

But then, this young bloke who had been loitering by the bar and who had been listening to my every word came over and said, "Toughest guy ha! Are you having a laugh? You're nothing but a fucking coward who hides behind your buddies when fighting ... as all hooligans do. That's why you always fight in packs."

I was gobsmacked by this sudden attack and went to hit him, but he ducked and the next thing I knew I was waking up in intensive care with a broken jaw and wired up to a drip.

It didn't take me long to discover the name of my attacker and when I did, Barry Gates said he would handle it and arrange for the firm to visit Sykes at his home address.   However, Sykes wasn't in. I had to laugh at that because I thought the guy was running scared knowing the Leeds Service Crew were after him and so I was amazed when I heard that the bastard had turned up at our local boozer, knocked out one of our lads, and taken over as top boy.

Indeed, I didn't believe it until I actually walked into the boozer and saw Sykes laughing and chatting with the rest of the firm. As soon as I did, the place went quiet because everybody knew he had put me in hospital and nobody knew how I would react.

Sykes didn't either and he put his pint down and came over and eyeballed me. "Do you have a fucking problem?" he said.

I did, but I didn't say so because I knew I couldn't beat him in a fight. I just shook my head and joined the rest of the lads at the bar.

I didn't stay with the firm long though, because I couldn't stand the man. Instead, I went and joined the army to get away from him and the rest of the mob. I didn't stay with Joanne Bickerstaff either, because after the fight she didn't want to know me and I suspect it was probably because she felt I was a loser and not the tough guy I had made myself out to be.

Still, I am not complaining. I spent 22 years in the army, and then left to work for Leeds Council, which I would not have done had I not met Paul Sykes. Had I not met him then God knows where I would be by now, because I had definitely been mixing with the wrong crowd as all hooligans do. So, in a weird way, meeting Sykes was a blessing in disguise albeit for the wrong reasons. The wrong reasons indeed.

DAVE HAMMOND

I was a member of Leeds United Service Crew back in 1962. Had I known that Billy Gates and the rest of the lads were going over to Wakefield to confront Paul Sykes for beating up Luke Thompson and putting him in hospital, I would have advised them against it. This is because I'm from Wakefield and knew Sykes very well as he went to the same senior school as me and he was certainly not a lad to piss about with. Unfortunately for them though, nobody told me as I was in bed with the flu ... and the rest, as they say, is history.

The first time I heard Paul Sykes' name was shortly after the start of the new school term in September 1957 when I was in the fourth year. Somebody told me that there was going to be a fight after school to determine who the cock of the first year was. I wasn't surprised about that because whenever kids start a new school there are always fights to see who is the hardest. But, I must admit my money was on his opponent winning, because that opponent was Trevor Flynn and he came from a family of hard knocks. Indeed, his brother Teddy was the cock of the second year and his brother Marcus was the cock of the school.

    It was a good job I didn't put money on Flynn winning though, because if I had I would have lost it. This is because Sykes not only won, but he also didn't even break into a sweat. He just walked up to his opponent and let forth a flurry of punches so fast that Flynn was left on the deck and out for the count in seconds.

  I was gobsmacked, as indeed was everybody else, and I thought for a moment that his brothers were going to have a go at him but they didn't. They just turned away in shock and knelt down and attended to their brother.

After that, rumours quickly abounded that the reason the brothers hadn't had a go at Sykes was because they were scared of fighting him. They knew they would lose if they did. Now I don't know if it was Sykes himself who spread the rumours, or if it was somebody else just stirring the pot, but it wasn't long before Teddy Flynn did challenge him to a fight. To be honest he had little choice, because with rumours circulating that he was afraid of fighting him what else could he do?

Still, he probably wished he hadn't because Sykes knocked him out just as easily as he had his brother. Everybody was shocked by that too, because nobody had ever heard of a first year beating the cock of the second year before. However, it wasn't over yet. Once Teddy had hit the floor and everybody had got over the shock of seeing him laid out there, the place went eerily silent as all eyes turned to Marcus, wondering what he was going to do about it.

In reality there was only one thing he could do, because the rumours were still circulating that he was frightened of fighting Sykes. Everybody knew if he didn't fight him, people really would think he was scared of him and as cock of the school, I doubted his ego would have allowed him to do so. This in fact turned out to be the case, because within seconds he and Sykes were laying into each other, and with a ferocity that surprised everybody watching.

They really tore into each other, and I thought Sykes had probably bitten off more than he could chew this time. Sykes was an eleven-year-old skinny kid of around five foot three, and Marcus was sixteen years old and five foot ten. How wrong I was ... because Sykes not only got the better of him, but also gave such a dazzling display of how to knock out an opponent much taller than you were, simply by pounding away at their head, body, and face that Muhammad Ali would have been proud of him.

Indeed Sykes gave such a dazzling display that it wasn't long before Marcus swayed on his feet, before hitting the floor. I stared at Sykes in amazement as I just could not believe that a first year kid was now the new cock of the school.

So, as I said earlier, if I had known that Billy Gates and the rest of the lads were going over to Wakefield to confront him for beating up Luke Thompson I would have advised them against it. Not only were they going up against one hard bastard; I doubted they would come off best no matter how many of them there were.

JOANNE BICKERSTAFF

I am the girl who was going out with Luke Thompson when Paul Sykes beat him up and put him in hospital and I can't say I was surprised, because I set the whole thing up and with good reason.

Luke Thompson was a two-timing son of a bitch who had been seeing other girls behind my back and he thought I would never get to hear of it. Only I did, because a friend of mine who worked over at Leeds hospital saw him in a nightclub one night with a blond in tow and wasted no time in telling me. I was fuming when I heard and was determined to get back at him so I did.

Luke was always bragging about how hard he was, and how he and his mates from the Leeds Service Crew were the hardest bastards around, that I decided to use it to my advantage and that is where Sykes came in.

I knew Sykes quite well as he used to come to my local and although he was a hit with many of the girls, he wasn't a hit with me. I don't quite know why that was because he was a good-looking lad with bulging muscles, but the fact remains he wasn't and as I say I can't quite explain it.

Still, that did not stop Sykes trying it on with me and trying to get me into bed and I can't blame him for that because back then I was quite a stunner. In fact I was so good-looking that my friends were always advising me to enter the Miss World contest. They used to say that if I had done, I would have won hands down. I never did though, as I was just too busy dating Luke and thinking what a nice guy he was. But, he wasn't, was he? He was a two-timing rat and I was determined to make him pay. So, as I said, I came up with a plan to make him do so, which involved Sykes and it was really quite simple.

I told Sykes that I would go to bed with him if he beat Luke up and put him in hospital. I lured Luke to the pub, got him to talk about the Leeds Service Crew and what a tough guy he was, knowing that Sykes would then challenge him to a fight, which would end with Luke winding up in intensive care just as I planned.

Luke Thompson was always saying the Leeds Service Crew were not lads to piss about with. Well that night he discovered that I wasn't a girl to piss about with either. It was as simple as that.

MIKE CROSSBY

I was a member of the Leeds Service Crew between 1971 and 1974 and although Paul Sykes had vanished from the hooligan scene by then, what with him being convicted of various offences and sent to prison many years earlier, it was clear that the man still held cult status amongst current and former hooligans by the way they spoke about him.

This became clear after I joined the firm because once I had been introduced to other members they quickly wasted no time in telling me about the things they got up to as hooligans and what they thought of the hooligan firms they had recently fought. To be honest it was fascinating stuff, because the thought of taking part in mass brawls against rival firms was why I had joined up in the first place. But, the best bit was when they told me about Sykes.

I had never heard of Sykes before, but afterwards I felt like I had known the man for years. It seemed everybody had a tale to tell about him even though many of them were only in their late teens and had never met him. So the stories they told me were ones which they had been told by somebody else and not which they had witnessed themselves. Nonetheless they were interesting to say the least.

One of my favourite stories involved a ruck that the Leeds Service Crew had against Southampton's firm, the appropriately named Scum Army, when Leeds were playing Southampton away in September 1962. This is because no sooner had the Leeds firm got off the train; they were attacked by the Southampton mob who began steaming into them with fists and boots, causing the Leeds mob to fall back in disarray.

Indeed, the Leeds mob were just about to turn and leg it when all of a sudden the Southampton mob froze and spun round as there was some commotion behind them and they weren't sure what it was. One of the Southampton lads told me many years later that he thought it was the police laying into them and trying to arrest them for a breach of the peace, but it wasn't. It was some lunatic with dark hair who he had never seen before but whom he later found out was called Paul Sykes.

Quite why Sykes was attacking them from the rear wasn't clear at the time, but it turned out to be over a girl. Apparently, when the train had pulled up at the station and the Leeds

Service Crew had jumped off, Sykes hadn't done so because he had been too busy giving his phone number to a girl he had taken a fancy to. He had, however, seen the Southampton mob attack his mates from the window and legged it down the train before getting off a carriage further down the platform and attacking them from the rear. To say they were surprised would be an understatement and it wasn't long before they had legged it down a tunnel, which connected one platform to another, and then out of the station. They were not seen again that day!

A second favourite story involved a ruck with Huddersfield's firm the Brackenhall Fine Casuals, which occurred in November 1962. It seemed Sykes was really looking forward to this as Huddersfield was only 15 miles from Dewsbury and if he could knock out their top boy his reputation as a hard man would be further cemented.

Sykes needn't have worried about his reputation, because in the hooligan world if you keep on beating boys as Sykes was doing, your reputation would spread far quicker than it takes you to say hey presto.

So, by the time Sykes and the rest of the Leeds Service Crew had turned up outside the local boozer where the Huddersfield firm were, Sykes' reputation had already spread well beyond the narrow confines of the Yorkshire Dales. So much so in fact, that their top boy, Raving Mike Razor – who'd got his name on account of the fact he liked to slash his opponents' faces with a razor – didn't want to know and refused to come outside and have a one to one with Sykesy as the latter demanded.

Even worse, the rest of Huddersfield's firm wouldn't have it out with the rest of the Leeds Service Crew either, as you would expect a rival hooligan firm to do, but instead they barricaded themselves in the pub and refused to come out. Everybody in the Leeds Service Crew was incensed by that because the whole point of being a football hooligan was to take on other football hooligans and show them who was boss.

We tried to kick the door down to get in but it was too well barricaded for that and in further desperation we smashed the windows in ... but it was a farce. The Huddersfield mob just beat us back with clubs and whatever other weapons they had when we tried to climb in, and we realised a new approach was needed.

That's when Sykesy had a stroke of genius.

What he did, was to leg it across the street and into the shop across the road. It was the day before Bonfire Night and the shop had fireworks for sale in their window. Sykes ran over and grabbed some, without bothering to pay, and began setting them off, aiming them at the smashed in pub windows.

The Huddersfield mob who had been watching his every move could not believe their eyes as fireworks started whizzing over their heads and exploding against the walls behind them. How anybody avoided getting injured let alone killed was anybody's guess, but it wasn't long before Raving Mike Razor was legging it out of the back along with the rest of the goons from his so-called hooligan mob, and looking somewhat astonished as they did.

But, my all-time favourite story regarding Sykes' hooligan days involved a ruck with Bury's firm the grand sounding Bury Riot Squad. This occurred in December 1962 and was one of those fights that took place behind a pub after Sykesy had challenged their top boy to a fight and the latter had been stupid enough to accept.

I say stupid, because even though he was the same size as Sykes and bulky with it, you wouldn't have thought so. This is because Sykes demolished him with such ease he didn't even break into a sweat. Just a left-right combination to his head, body and face, and the man was down in a blink of an eye.

The Bury mob were aghast and wanted to do a runner, but there was nowhere for them to run to as there was nothing but a large wall behind them. So Sykes knocked another of them out, followed by another and then another and he then asked if any of the others wanted to fight him. They didn't, and they all looked away not wanting to catch his eye in case he punched them next. In fact what they wanted to do was scarper, but as I said there was nowhere for them to go. Instead, they continued to avoid Sykesy's gaze as he stood there glaring at them menacingly.

Eventually he tired of it all and got them to sing Baa Baa Black Sheep, which to my surprise they did. After he had relieved them of any money they had on them for putting on such a pathetic show, he walked away, with the Bury mob, singing Baa Baa Black Sheep.

JOE FRAZIER

Hi, I'm Joe Frazier; or Smokin' Joe Frazier as I am widely known, and I was the undisputed Heavyweight Champion of the World between 1970 and 1973.

I first met Paul Sykes when I flew over to England to fight Joe Bugner in July 1973. Sykes was chosen to be one of my sparring partners so I could accustom myself to the British climate and get in shape before the fight.

To say Sykes was an exceptional fighter would be an understatement, because he was more than that. He was the best sparring partner I have ever had and to be honest I found it hard to lay a punch on him. Not only that but even when I did he just soaked it up as though it had no effect. Even more surprising, he had the best, left right combination I have ever come across and with his enormous strength, I was very lucky not to hit the deck before the ref called time.

It was embarrassing to say the least. I was supposed to be the Heavyweight Champion of the World, and the best fighter around, and yet here was this unknown boxer from Wakefield putting me in my place and giving me a lesson in boxing that I would never forget. To be honest though, I was also really annoyed because we were sparring in front of the world's press, and anybody watching could not help but notice that I was out of my depth and fighting a man who was a better fighter than me, even though I was World Champion.

To my relief though, none of the press thought I was fighting to my best ability but instead was simply larking about for the benefit of the cameras and so nothing was said in the papers and the matter passed unnoticed.

When I got back to the States after beating Bugner and retaining my crown, I phoned Sykesy and congratulated him on giving me what I thought was the best sparring session I had ever had. What's more I invited him to fly out to America to join me in my gym and help me prepare for my fight against Mohammed Ali, who at the time was telling anyone who would listen that he was going to challenge me to a fight and become the Heavyweight Champion of the world for the second time in his life.

Much to my delight, Sykes did come over and during the following weeks I got to know him well. I have to say, the man was a mean, lean fighting machine in every sense of the word. He could punch, he could box, he had phenomenal strength, he was everything a good boxer should be, and though he did not knock me out, he came very close to doing so once or twice I can assure you.

One of the things I really liked about Sykes however, was the stories he used to tell me about his football hooligan days when we were relaxing in the bar across the road. Sykes was a member of the Leeds Service Crew who were a bunch of football hooligans that used to follow Leeds United around the country but only to fight other football hooligans and show them who was the hardest.

To be honest, I wasn't surprised that such things went on in England, even though it is often thought to be the most civilised country in the world, because here in America we have a similar thing with baseball teams attracting their own hooligan following. Sounds pathetic I know, but boys like to be boys and like to fight and show they are the hardest, which is after all why I became a boxer and the Heavyweight Champion of the World.

One of the best stories I heard about Sykes' hooligan days, involved Swansea City's firm the Swansea Jack Army, which struck me as a weird name. It turned out that their top boy was known as Mad Jack Lewyyn so I guess it must have been named after him. Anyway, this Mad Jack went storming into the Leeds firm with the rest of his crew behind him and it wasn't long before fists and boots were flying in all directions. Sykesy of course was in the thick of it and enjoying every moment even though he was having problems getting to Mad Jack. Every time he tried to, some bozo got in his way and he had to deal with them first.

Eventually though, Sykes fought his way through and hit Mad Jack so hard the guy flew through the air and was out for the count. He then took his hat as a souvenir, which he later gave to me.

You may not believe this, but when Rocky came out in 1976 and thousands of cinemagoers saw the main protagonist Apollo Creed entering the ring wearing his shorts, coat, and top hat, it was the same top hat that Sykes had stolen from Mad Jack all those years before. I kid you not … because I was the one who had given it to Sylvester Stallone himself to use in his movie.

Another story involved Chelsea's firm, the infamous Chelsea Headhunters and this was a farce from start to finish.

In those days, trains from Leeds to London took an astonishing nine hours and by the time they reached London, most of the Leeds Service Crew were so pissed they did not get off the train in London and wound up in Plymouth on the south coast. Sykes was fuming as one of the lads was a strict Methodist and had promised to wake them when they got to London, but the stupid bastard fell asleep and didn't wake them up. Furious, Sykes forced him to drink large amounts of booze, despite his religious beliefs banning the consumption of alcohol, and by the time he got back to Leeds the poor lad was so pissed he didn't get off the train with the rest of them. He remained where he was until he was awoken by a guard over 179 miles away in Glasgow.

But the best story about Paul Sykes' hooligan days did not take place during those days but as a consequence of it.

I've never told anybody this before, partly because I doubted anybody would have believed me, and partly because Mohammed Ali would have called me a liar and sued me for slander knowing I could not prove it even though it was true and it really did happen. Still Ali is dead now and therefore cannot sue me and so I will tell it to you.

 The story in question took place during the second week of Sykesy's visit when I was sparring with him late one evening in the gym. We were having a good session and as usual I was once again marvelling at how good a fighter the man was when I heard somebody banging on the door. When I opened it, Mohammed Ali was standing there with a big cheesy grin on his face.

 He said, with a slight twinkle in his eye, "Hi Joe, how's it going? I was just visiting the area, so I thought I would pay you a visit."

I flinched, because although I had huge respect for him as a fighter, I never did like him much as a person. To me, the man was a loud-mouthed bully who liked to harass and intimidate people in order to get his way, both inside and outside the ring. But before I could say anything more however, he had just pushed past me and into the building.

I was fuming but I didn't chuck him out, because that would have created more problems than it solved, what with his ego being as big as it was. Instead, I asked him what he wanted because men like Ali always wanted something. They don't just call upon you to see how you are doing because that is not in their nature. They do it because they want something from you ... in this case it was information. He wanted to know something about George Foreman who at the time was knocking out all before him.

So, after I had updated him on what it was he wanted to know he turned to Sykesy and said with another grin on his face, "Now who is this Joe? Your whipping boy?"

I had to laugh at that because the idea that Sykes was anybody's whipping boy was just too ridiculous to contemplate.

In normal circumstances, Sykes would have punched anybody who said that. However, in this case he stood looking on at Ali in awe. It was hardly surprising because Ali was the most famous boxer in the world at the time, as he still is now, and a living legend in every sense of the word. So naturally he was in awe of seeing him.

That said, I told Ali that Sykes was the hardest man in Britain, as well as the infamous leader of Leeds Service Crew who had once fought four Liverpool hooligans at the same time and knocked them all out.

Ali was so impressed when he heard that, he asked if he could do a few rounds with Sykes. After the latter had agreed to it, looking mesmerised by it all as he did, I showed Ali the changing rooms and kitted him out with boxing gear as he had not brought any himself.

About ten minutes later, I found myself in the middle of the ring about to referee a sparring bout between Mohammed Ali and Paul Sykes. There was nobody else in the gym and to be honest I had to pinch myself this was really happening because the whole thing seemed surreal to me. Sykesy too seemed taken aback by it all, and looked at me as though he still could not believe what was going on. But Ali was just leaning against the ropes with a cocky grin on his face waiting for the session to begin and looking as though he was about to enjoy himself at Sykes' expense.

As soon as the bout began, Ali continued to give that impression because instead of squaring up to his opponent with his fists raised as boxers do, he started to dance around him and taunt him in the process. Sykesy wasn't amused and smashed a fist into his face, which sent Ali crashing to the ground, and looking very sorry for himself. I had to laugh at that because it wasn't what Ali was expecting, nor me either to be brutally honest, and the look on Ali's face was comical. But he had brought it on himself by not taking Sykes seriously and even taking the mickey out of him and that was a stupid thing to do, a very stupid thing to do indeed.

Ali got to his feet and moved towards Sykes with a lot more seriousness than he had before and in no time at all was laying into him with a flurry of punches to the head, body and face, which sent Sykes wheeling back and putting his fists in front of his head in order to soak up the punches and prevent Ali doing any real damage. Ali was giving it all he had and I wasn't surprised by that because Sykes had decked him with one punch and nobody in history had ever done that to him before, not even Sonny Liston who was said to have the hardest punch in history.

Still Sykesy was a giver not a taker and so it wasn't long before he was smashing his fists into Ali's face and giving as good as he got. Indeed, he was putting up such a good show that I just stood there looking on and thinking that this was better than watching some of the World Heavyweight fights I had seen. I was so taken with how good a fight it was, that I nearly forgot that I was the referee and that this was only a sparring session. So, I quickly got my act together and over the next ten minutes I spent a lot of my time telling them to back off, quickly pulling them apart when they wound up in a clinch, or saying time out and giving them a short break.

That said, these two were fighters and were determined to get the better of each other, even though they couldn't. But Sykes was a hooligan and not just a boxer, so before I knew it he had headbutted Ali with such force the man hit the deck and was out for the count.

Ali was fuming when he came to and he left the gym in a right huff. But because he did not want people to know Sykes had beaten him, he never said anything. His ego was too big for that.

As for Sykes he never said anything either, not even when he published his bestselling autobiography, *Sweet Agony*, and I don't know why he did that, unless it was because like me he feared Ali would deny it and sue him for slander. But whatever the reason it was probably for the best, because Sykes was a football hooligan with a reputation for extreme violence, and I doubt anybody would have believed he had beaten Mohammed Ali in a one-to-one fight, do you?

FORMER POLICE OFFICER

Unlike everybody else in this book, I am not going to do anything or say anything that may help the police identify me. This is because my dealings with Paul Sykes were not exactly on the level, even though I was a serving police officer and it was my job to uphold the law. Indeed, it is for this reason that I did not give my name to the author when I rang and asked him if he would like to interview me for this book, which I had heard he was writing on the grapevine. He said yes, and the interview took place on the phone with me using an untraceable mobile, so nobody could find me that way. In fact the mobile is now languishing at the bottom of the Leeds and Liverpool canal in order to prevent them from doing so.

That said; my dealings with Sykes came about not because of his hooligan activities but because of my interest in photography, which I had developed since I was a boy. This is because I was in Leeds city centre taking pictures of the famous buildings that lined its streets when I heard a large commotion behind me and saw this vicious looking youth beating the hell out of another youth. What's more, my heart missed a beat because although I had never met him, I knew who the vicious looking youth was because I had recently been appointed a Detective Constable at Wakefield Police Station, and his face was plastered all over the notice board. So, as quick as a flash I took a picture of him as he continued to lay into his opponent, before the sound of police sirens filled the air and he did a runner leaving his victim lying in a pool of blood and very much the worse for wear.

I didn't stay around to inform my colleagues in Leeds that I had witnessed the attack, or that I had captured it on camera and could identify the perpetrator, because I had other plans for Sykes. I knew from what I had heard about him that he was not only the leader of the Leeds Service Crew, but that many of his firm came from Wakefield – he had persuaded a lot of them to join his firm and provide it with extra muscle. I wanted to use the picture to blackmail him and get him to pass on information about his mates to me, particularly as I knew many of them were drug dealers, or other lowlife scumbags.

It worked, because as soon as I showed him the picture he was only too willing to grass his mates up, rather than go to prison, as most football hooligans end up doing. This is why various members of his firm were arrested during the course of the next few months, with their crimes ranging from drug dealing, to wounding with intent, and even armed robbery. In the case of the latter, we actually waited for the perpetrator to show up at the bank, and when he did and tried to rob the place, he was arrested on the spot thanks to the information given to us by Sykes.

It was fantastic stuff and my bosses at the station were so delighted that I was promoted to Detective Sergeant and Detective Inspector not long after that. But my dealings with Sykes did not last long, because the stupid bastard got himself nicked for a crime I could not cover up, and which led to him getting banged up and unable to pass on information about his dodgy mates to me.

I was fuming; as indeed was Sykes who threatened to report me to my bosses for blackmailing him if I didn't get him off the charge. I just laughed and said go ahead. I told him it was his word against mine, and whom did he think people would believe ... a serving police officer – with an unblemished record – or a vicious criminal with a history of violence? What's more, I told him that once his mates in prison found out he was a grass his life wouldn't be worth living, and he could end up with a knife in his back. It did not matter how hard he was, and how feared he was because that's what happened to grasses in prison. They tended to get knifed and by the very people they themselves had knifed in order to avoid being sent to prison in the first place.

MISS BARBARA WHIPLASH

I was the leader of Ipswich's firm the Ipswich Punishment Squad (IPS) in the early fifties and knew most of the naughty boys in the hooligan world, either by reputation or because I had met them personally. Thugs like Bobby the Wolf for example, who was not only the legendary leader of West Ham's infamous Intercity Firm, but also my friend and lover. However, it wasn't because of my hooligan activities that I met Paul Sykes, but through a mutual friend who brought Sykes to a sex party I was holding at a house outside Wakefield in 2001.

To be honest I was horrified when I saw him, because he was clearly living rough and could do with a good bath. But the person who had brought him said he was a local celebrity and I might find him interesting and I certainly did that.

What I found interesting about Sykes was that not only had he been a formidable street fighter in his day and held the title of the hardest prisoner in Britain, but was also a former football hooligan and had some interesting tales to tell. One of which involved a ruck he had had with the Bristol firm the infamous Bristol Gas Squad in April 1962.

What happened there was that Sykes, who was the leader of the Leeds Service Crew, was walking home with the rest of his firm, when the Bristol Gas Squad pulled up in a van and began charging at them with baseball bats. Sykes was annoyed when firms did that because he always thought it was a cowardly way of settling disputes and that grown men should settle their disputes with their fists and nothing else. In a way I admired him for that because it was a gentleman's way of doing things and very much the way they did things in Victorian times with gangs settling their disputes with their bare fists.

Still, as it happened, luck was on Sykes' side because one particular thug came charging towards him, but then fell over in his rush to get to him, dropping his baseball bat in the process. Sykes just picked it up and smashed it into his face so hard, he flew through the air and crashed into the van that had brought him, causing his mates to flee in panic at the sight. Sykes then relieved the unconscious man of his wallet, before treating himself and the rest of his firm to a slap-up meal at his expense, once they got back to Wakefield.

Another story involved Cardiff's firm the Soul Crew. They turned up in Leeds over a hundred strong and sneaked up to the pub where Sykes and the rest of his firm were drinking, hoping to take them by surprise. What the Cardiff mob didn't realise
was that this was a trap, and the Leeds firm were waiting for them with some Rottweilers in tow – which is why they had not posted any spotters outside to stop them sneaking up to the pub in the first place.

As soon as they burst in, they saw Sykes and the rest of the Leeds firm grinning at them, before they let the Rottweilers off their leads. They then watched in amusement as the dogs chased the Soul Crew down the street. They stood there laughing as the stupid bozos jumped into a nearby canal in order to escape the dogs and nearly getting mowed down by a canal barge in the process.

That was funny, but the best story involved Sykes' run-in with the Everton County Road Cutters which took place in October 1962. What happened was that Sykes and the rest of his mob turned up outside their ground only to find Everton's firm waiting for them in large numbers and with a couple of girls with them for good measure. Although it was very unusual for hooligans to bring their girlfriends with them, it was not unheard of. This was because sometimes the girlfriends liked to see grown men fight or even liked to take part in fights themselves.

This was certainly the case on this occasion, because one of the girls, a spotty faced girl of around nineteen, suddenly stepped forward and pointing at Paul said, "You're the Leeds top boy and I'm Everton's top girl! How about it ... you and me have a one to one?"

She then started jumping up and down and doing a bit of shadow boxing in the process, making her look a right prat as she did.

Sykes just smiled and said he would love to have a one to one with her, but in the bedroom not there, which led to Everton's top boy stepping forward and taking a swing at him. Sykes, however, just ducked and then punched the guy so hard in the face he tumbled backwards and hit the deck clearly unconscious.

At that, the rest of the mob turned and fled except the girl, who was looking at Sykes in awe at what he had just done and how quickly he had done it. The next thing everybody in his firm knew was she started kissing him passionately on the lips and begged him to take her back to his room for sex.

That was Sykes through and through. A man who liked the ladies and never missed an opportunity to have sex with them as his autobiography shows.

Anyway, back to my party... while I had been talking to Sykes, he had been eyeing up all the naked waitresses; and pinching them on their bottoms even though he did not have the money to pay for sex. So, I took him into a room and whipped his backside for being the very naughty he was, and always had been.

CHARLIE (BROADMOOR PATIENT)

I was in the hospital wing of Broadmoor in the 1970s recovering from a serious bout of pneumonia when in walked a bunch of orderlies pushing this guy on a trolley who didn't look well. In fact he looked as sick as a parrot and at first I thought he was a resident of the nut house, as Broadmoor was generally known, but he wasn't. He was a Category A prisoner who had fallen ill while being transferred from one prison to another and needed urgent medical treatment.

They had brought him there instead of the nearest hospital, which was only a mile away as the place was better equipped and better protected to deal with nutters like him, or at least that is what I overheard one of his prison guards telling an orderly when they questioned why he had been brought there.

Over the next few days I got to know Sykes very well, because he was in the bed next to me while the doctors treated him for whatever illness was ailing him. Right from the start it was obvious that Sykes was a man who liked to talk about himself and his past in general. He asked me what my name was and I told him it was Charlie. He then began telling me about football hooligans; and the problems he had had with them in prison over the years.

One story involved hooligans from Hull City's firm, the Hull City Psychos, who were inside Walton nick in Merseyside when Sykes was there back in the seventies.

They had been sent to Walton for violent affray and as soon as they arrived, they discovered they were on the same wing as hooligans from Liverpool's firm, the infamous Liverpool Urchins.

Now normally this would not have been a problem, because when football hooligans go to prison they tend to get on rather well with other football hooligans. This is because they have a lot in common and know the same people. But, on this occasion there was a lot of bad blood between them because during a previous encounter, one of the Hull City Psychos had stabbed one of the Urchins, killing him instantly and sending him to an early grave. Although the person who had pulled out the knife, and stabbed his opponent, was serving a life sentence on the Isle of Wight, the Liverpool firm still wanted revenge. The lad who had been killed was none other than Terry Watkins, the twin brother of Liverpool's top boy Danny Watkins and Danny was not a person to cross.

So, the Hull lads were worried because Walton was full of Scousers with links to the Liverpool firm and if a fight broke out, they would almost certainly lose. They went to Sykesy to enlist his support, which on the face of it was a good move because Sykesy was not only the hardest prisoner in Walton but also in the entire prison system. He was also a Yorkshire lad and so they thought he would take their side, what with them being Yorkshire lads too.

However, Sykes didn't want to know. He said if they were cowardly enough to use weapons to settle disputes then they should be manly enough to settle those disputes on their own.

So, he left them to do just that which didn't turn out very well for them. As I said, the place was full of people with links to the Liverpool firm, what with the prison being situated in an area of Liverpool itself, so when a fight broke out in the yard the Liverpool mobbed destroyed the Hull mob in minutes, and ended up stabbing their top boy in the process.

On another occasion, Sykes had a run in with Bolton's firm the Cuckoo Boys and this was one of those fights that happened by accident rather than by design.

Both firms were in Manchester as Leeds were playing Manchester City away, and Bolton were playing their local rivals Manchester United away and, as such, each of them was expecting to do battle with one of the Manchester firms. However, things turned into a farce when one of the Bolton mob spotted the Leeds Crew, and despite the fact that both of them were wearing their teams' shirts, which were white and neither City or United played in white, the stupid bastards went steaming into each other thinking they were fighting the Manchester firm they were expecting to be fighting that day.

So, punch after punch was thrown, as was kick after kick, but still nobody realised that the firm they were fighting was not the firm they were expecting to fight. But then, one of the Bolton lads suddenly saw Leeds United plastered over somebody's shirt and yelled, "Whoa, who the fuck are you lot? You're not Manchester United's firm are you?"

"We're the Leeds Service Crew," said Sykes, punching a yob senseless and then turning to him with a scowl on his face. "Who the fuck do you think we are? Isn't that obvious from our shirts?"

Well, one of the Bolton lads took offence to that and made some reference about Sykes being too thick to notice they were wearing Bolton shirts and even called him a dipstick. So, Sykes just went over and knocked him out with one punch, unaware that both the City and Man United firms were watching and laughing, and thinking what a bunch of prats they were, for assuming they were fighting one of the Manchester firms.

But the thing I remember best about Sykes was the way he used to harp on about football hooliganism and how it used to attract some of the most dangerous lunatics in the country, from Bobby the Wolf of West Ham fame, to his notorious counterpart at Millwall, Harry the Dog.

Sykes loved reading their books and thought they were some of the best hooligan books around, what with their violence and the hooligans' complete disregard for authority of any kind. He was particularly fascinated with Jackson Frane, the Reading Nightmare, and how he managed to remain a football hooligan for over forty years, despite the number of stabbings, shootings and fist fights he was involved in. Sykes rated his autobiography *Nightmare* the best hooligan book of them all.

Just before he was transferred back to prison he shook my hand and said, "Remember this Charlie ... that football hooliganism tends to attract the nutters, and I mean the nutters."

"I know," I replied sardonically. "I was a football hooligan myself back in the fifties and I met a few of them."

"You were?" Sykes was shocked. "You never told me that. What firm did you run with?"

"Blackburn's Mill Hill Mob," I said with a grin. "I was their top boy."

Sykes smiled and then gasped. "What's your full name?" he choked.

"Charlie … Charlie McFudden."

Sykes went completely white. "Bloody hell," he said, "you're the guy, who chopped off the heads of Burnley hooligans with a chainsaw and stuck them on the gates of the ground afterwards, aren't you? Back in the fifties? The one they refer to as Chainsaw Charlie?"

"I am indeed," I said, with a widening grin. "And you're right football hooliganism does bring out the nutters. Some right bloody nutters. This is why I have been in the nuthouse for over thirty years and will remain here until the day I die. Or at least that's what the judge said when I was certified insane and sent here."

FATHER JOHN WILKINS

I was the priest at St Peter the Martyrs Catholic Church in Wakefield for over forty years and knew Paul Sykes very well. He would often come to the church between 2005 and 2007, the final years of his life, to pray or have a chat.

When he came he would often tell me about his hooligan days and some of the things he got up during those days that involved the church. On one occasion for example, he told me how he had chased a couple of Derby hooligans behind the church and given them a right beating for their troubles. There were three of them against just him, but he knocked them out with a series of lightning blows that would have made Bruce Lee proud, before helping himself to their wallets and going down the road to get pissed at the pub. He did the same to a Liverpool fan who had pulled a knife out on him in the graveyard, before jumping up and down on his head for good measure.

I wasn't happy about that because I am against violence as you can imagine, and said as much to Sykes, but he just accused me of being a hypocrite.

He said nobody in the history of Britain had engaged in more violence than the Catholic Church. He said I shouldn't be too quick to condemn him for attacking rival football hooligans when the church had been engaged in violent campaigns for centuries, as witnessed by the Inquisition, and Salem Witch Hunts. Indeed, he said that during these events the church had often ordered its adherents to engage in mass killings, large executions, and vast purges of anybody the church classed as a threat, whether it be because of their religious, political, or social beliefs.

Now I was taken aback by that because I wouldn't have thought Sykes would have been so knowledgeable about such things, but I later discovered that he was actually a very clever man with a master's degree in social history. Still, before I could say anything he went on to say that the church and football hooligans had a lot in common.

   I just turned to him and said, "Rubbish!"

   But, he then went to list what these similarities were. First, he said, the church had a history of meting out punishment on those within its organisation who did not obey its top boy on earth, which in the church's case was the Pope. He said that when he was top boy of the Leeds Service Crew he regularly beat up any member of the firm he did not see eye to eye with, but that was nothing compared to the Pope.

During the Middle Ages the Pope had labelled those who questioned his authority as heretics and had them burned at the stake, as he did in 1584 for example, when the Catholic Bishops, James Bell and John Finch were burned in Lancaster for questioning the authority of Pope Gregory XIII in that year.

Secondly, he said that the church, like football hooligans, was not only violent to those who were members of its own firm so to speak, but to those who weren't. As witnessed in 1555, when Pope Paul IV had the Protestant martyrs Hugh Latimer, Nicholas Ridley, and John Hooper, burned at the stake for questioning the authority of the Catholic Church in England. This was not unlike football hooligans who regularly beat up those from other firms who questioned their authority. However, nobody ever got burned at the stake, although

Liverpool's top Boy Uriah Thomas, did burn West Ham's top boy Bobby the Wolf alive in a coffin back in 1952.

Finally, Sykes said the church expected everybody to believe in its ultimate top boy which was God. He said that in the Bible it refers to an event called the rapture, where all the people on earth who believe in God are teleported to heaven and given a peaceful and joyous life, whereas those who don't believe in God, are left to rot on earth and suffer endless torment. That, he said, was no different to football hooligans who liked to see their opponents suffer endless torment too if they didn't believe in them.

This was the weirdest conversation I have ever had during my time as a priest, and Sykes was the weirdest person I had ever met. But Sykes died not long after this and the question of whether football hooligans and the Catholic Church had a lot in common is something that often plagues me to this day. Was he right? I don't know, but I know one thing, the behaviour of the Catholic Church in the past did leave an awful lot to be desired, and I mean an awful lot to be desired.

MICHAELA CRANE

I'm Michaela Crane and back in the seventies I was known as the Governess, that is Britain's hardest woman and the Chelsea Headhunters' top girl. It may surprise you that a girl was a football hooligan, and a leading member of the Chelsea mob, but it's true and you can read all about it in my autobiography, *Michaela Crane, The Shocking Story of Britain's Hardest Female Football Hooligan*, which is available on Amazon, and currently number one on its bestseller list.

My dealings with Paul Sykes however, did not come about because of my hooligan activities but because I attended a British National Party (BNP) rally in August 2003. The BNP were protesting at the number of unwashed scumbags who were setting up home in the city, after arriving there from Pakistan or whatever hellhole they had come from. Indeed, I had a lot of sympathy for the BNP because as far back as the 1970s, my cousin Mickey and I ran security for the British Movement (BM) which was not only the most violent neo-Nazi group in British history, but one which sought to create a Nazi dictatorship in Britain by expelling all non-white scumbags back to where they had came from.

So, I first became aware of Sykes when I noticed this dishevelled man in his fifties, clutching a beer can in his hand and talking to that notorious scumbag Andi Ali.   Back in the eighties, Ali was known as the hardest Asian in the country after winning a series of unlicensed bouts up and down the land, even though he failed to mention this in that utter crap book of his, *Dead Paki Walking*. Instead he harps on about how he became the number one target on a BNP hit list called Redwatch after ignoring death threats to stop his academic research on the BNP, which to be fair he had. However, it still annoyed me that he was there taking pictures and interviewing people for his research, because it seemed to me that he was sticking two fingers up to me and everyone else in the BNP. It was as if he was saying; well okay you have put me on a neo-Nazi hit list, so here I am ... what are you going to do about it?

Indeed, I was so angry about it I said as much to my cousin Mickey. But to my astonishment he was more interested in the man Ali was talking to, rather than Ali himself.

"Do you know who that man is?" he asked, turning to me with surprise.

"No," I said, puzzled. "Who is he?"

"Paul Sykes."

I stared at him. "What *the* Paul Sykes? The Paul Sykes who was classed as the hardest prisoner in the seventies?"

Mickey nodded.

"Christ," I said. "The man looks a right bloody wreck doesn't he? A right bloody wreck."

Still, I never got the chance to talk to Sykes that day because just then the local BNP organiser began making a speech and by the time he had finished Sykes had disappeared. I would never see him again, as he died shortly afterwards of alcohol abuse.

In a way it upset me because after seeing him at the rally I realised that I had met him before, but not for over thirty years however, which was why I had not recognised him at first. I could not class him as a friend, but our paths had crossed back in the seventies because he used to come to Joey Porter's gym to spar with Roy Shaw. At the time, Shaw was considered to be the hardest man in the country, and held the title of Governor to prove it.

Indeed, Porter used to bring Sykes down from Wakefield for that very purpose and the only people who Porter ever brought in to be sparring partners for Shaw, were people who really could fight and give Shaw a run for his money. Sykes could certainly do that.

I was there when Sykes, in fact, hammered Shaw and put him down so many times it was painful to watch. Shaw didn't like it of course, and kept getting up and laying into Sykes like a Rottweiler off his leash, but it did him no good because Sykes just soaked it all up before knocking him out for good measure.

Years later when Shaw wrote his number-one bestseller, *Pretty Boy*, he portrayed himself as a mean, lean, fighting machine who nobody could beat, and he boasted he was the hardest man in the country. He was not. Sykes was harder and when Shaw came to after Sykes had knocked him out; he started kicking off and saying it was a lucky punch.

Sykes just grabbed him by the throat and threw him out the back door saying, "Oh yeah, you think it was a lucky punch do you? Well how about a one-to-one fight now? No rules, no gloves, just you and me."

Well Shaw didn't want to do that as I could see by the fear in his eyes and to my astonishment, he started crying and pleading for Sykes not to hurt him.

Sykes just knocked him out anyway, before turning round to everybody and saying, "Look, I've knocked him out again and when he comes round I want you to ask him if that was a lucky punch too. If he says yes, let me know and I will be back to give him another lucky punch."

With that, he stormed out of the gym leaving everybody staring after him in disbelief including both Mickey and me.

Shaw might have been terrified of fighting Paul Sykes, despite the fact he was supposed to be the hardest man in the country, but one man who was not afraid to fight Sykes was Lee Duffy and with good reason.

Duffy was a right bruiser and the hardest man in Middlesbrough. He had a history of violence that rivalled Sykes'. Indeed, he was a former football hooligan who in his late teens had run with the Middlesbrough Frontline, and, like Sykes, had become his firm's top boy when he was just sixteen years old.

However, Duffy never got to meet Sykes during his hooligan days because he was born in 1965, and by that time Sykes' hooligan days were long over.

The fight between Sykes and Duffy came about after the two clashed in Durham Prison in 1989. What happened was Duffy, who was the top dog in the prison, was challenged by Sykes who had been sent there for beating up four bouncers the night before. The moment Sykes saw Duffy he punched him so hard in the face that he hit the ground and was out for the count. What's more, when Duffy came round he started crying like a baby. The screw who told me this, said the scene was quite comical really because Duffy was always dressed in shorts and throwing his weight about, but there he was, sitting there on the floor wailing like a little baby in his shorts. Indeed, the screw said it was hard to believe that this was the infamous Lee Duffy who had struck fear into the hearts of many. But, it was and as the screw said, it was unbelievable ... totally unbelievable.

Duffy never got the chance to go after Sykes again in prison because he was released the very next day and he had to wait until Sykes came out of prison to do so. By that time, Joey Porter had got involved and arranged for them to take part in an unlicensed bare-knuckle fight at a gypsy campsite on the outskirts of York.

I travelled up to the fight with my cousin Mickey, and as soon as I saw Duffy I was struck by what an odd-looking fella he was, because he had the weirdest shaped head I have seen in my life, and I mean the weirdest shaped head.

Still, he came at Sykes with all guns blazing, and hit him with a lovely smack to his face which sent him wheeling backwards looking gobsmacked. Quite what he was looking so gobsmacked about I had no idea, because in a fight you should expect to receive a punch or two. However, he quickly recovered and was soon trading blow after blow and headbutt after headbutt.

   To be honest I was surprised Sykes was taking so long to finish him, because it had never taken him this long to finish an opponent before. As the fight rumbled on with fists and boots flying in all directions, I started to wonder if perhaps he was ever going to win the fight at all. Judging by the looks on the faces of many of Sykes' supporters, they were wondering this too. They were clearly shocked by his lacklustre performance. Looking back, I put it down to two reasons. The first was that Sykes was by then forty-three years old, and past his prime, and the second was Duffy was only twenty-five and could handle himself well despite getting knocked out by Sykes in an earlier rout.

Duffy was getting in a lot of good punches and clearly had some boxing skills. We watched as he hit Sykes in the stomach before pounding away at his ribs and then shooting up with an upper crust, which connected with his chin sending him wheeling back and almost tumbling to the ground. I say almost, because Sykes somehow managed to stay on his feet. How he did so neither I nor anybody else in the crowd had the faintest idea. With the crowd urging the fighters on you could feel the tension in the air.

Like many, I was now convinced Sykes was going to lose particularly as Duffy managed to land a couple more punches to his head, body and face, and then headbutted Sykes with such force he had blood pouring out of his nose. But then, Duffy made the mistake of relaxing his guard too soon, possibly because he thought Sykes was too dazed to fight back; or possibly because he was becoming too cocky. However, the next thing I knew Sykes had given him such a right-hander that Duffy flew through the air and hit the deck unconscious.

It happened so fast and against the run of play that for a moment there was just silence. But then, Jackie Riley, Harry the Dog's girlfriend, ran over and removed Duffy's shorts from him, before waving them in the air and shouting, "Souvenirs of the fight anyone?"

At that, everybody burst out laughing including Duffy's own mates.

Duffy wasn't laughing when he heard about it though and wanted revenge on her. However, Harry the Dog simply warned him that if he ever went near her he would blow his head off with a shotgun. Anyone who knew Harry knew he wasn't joking.

After the fight, Duffy was fuming that Sykes had knocked him out and demanded a rematch, but it never came to anything. This was because a few weeks later, Duffy was killed when he got into a fight with some former football hooligan from Middlesbrough, who knifed him to death and was later arrested for murder. He was actually found not guilty, after a court decided he had acted in self-defence, but the result was that Duffy and Sykes never had a rematch. Whether he would have beaten Sykes is anybody's guess. I know what I think. What about you?

FINAL NOTE FROM THE AUTHOR

These are just some of the stories about Paul Sykes' hooligan days. They are written by those who had known Sykes during those days or in his later life, or had heard about them, either from Sykes himself or from his fellow hooligans. They are the stories of people who fought with him both on and off the terraces and who witnessed at first hand the invincible fighting machine that Sykes was. People such as Michaela Crane, for example, or the notorious Miss Barbara Whiplash.

Perhaps the best story about Sykes, however, is the one that has so far not been told. Namely, why did Jamie Boyle not mention in his book *The Whole of the Moon*, that Lee Duffy had fought Paul Sykes and lost? To me that is one of the most amazing things about Jamie Boyle's book, particularly as Boyle has written some rather good books on Sykes. He does not mention the fight in any of his books.

Still, all I will say is the best way to find out why Jamie Boyle did not mention the Sykes verses Duffy fight is to join him on one of his regular podcasts and ask him. I would be very interested to hear his answer, and I mean very interested.

Gussy Gassam
Wakefield
2022.

Printed in Great Britain
by Amazon

The Nightmare Call

© **Alan Derwi**

To my old buddy Jason M with amusement.

INTRODUCTION

Since the publication of my number one bestseller, *Nightmare*, I have been inundated by people asking if I was going to write a sequel and if so when. Most of these requests have been made by people who did not know the Nightmare personally, but were nonetheless fascinated by his many street fights, prison punch-ups and hooligan encounters, outlined in the book. Other requests have simply been made by those who knew the Nightmare personally and had interesting stories to tell about him.

This book is a collection of those stories, written both by those who have witnessed at first hand the violent exploits of the legend that is the

Nightmare and by those who have heard stories about him.

    Alan Derwi
    Reading
    February 2022

TEDDY MITSKER

I first came across the Nightmare in September 1966, when we both started Waterfield Senior School in Reading. He wasn't in my class but he soon made his presence known because he challenged my best mate Keven Peacock to a fight.

Peacock wasn't just a tough kid with a fierce reputation, but at six foot four, he was one of the biggest kids in the school; even though he was just a first year and not yet twelve years old. He towered over the rest of us and what made Frane think he could beat someone who was fourteen inches taller than he was at the time was anybody's guess. But he did think he could and it was a rather foolish thing to do, because Peacock just walked over and knocked him out with one punch.

That was quite funny when I come to think of it, but anybody who thought Frane was a weakling was in for a shock. He started to knock out all the other hard cases in the first year, sending them tumbling to the ground, and booting them in the head for good measure. Indeed, he made it look so easy that everybody said that if Peacock and Frane had been the same height, then Frane would have beaten Peacock hands down.

I tend to agree with that assessment because Frane was the most vicious bastard I have ever seen. In fact, Frane was a psychopath and didn't seem to have respect for anybody at school, not even the teachers.

I can remember on one occasion seeing a teacher in tears, because he had given her hell for taking one kid's side over his. He had punched that kid in the face for no apparent reason and then went as far as to suggest that the teacher was only sticking up for him because she was engaged in a sexual relationship with him. It was all bullshit of course and Frane knew it, but he also knew that mud sticks, and rumours such as that would fly around the school in no time, making the teacher's life hell. As a result of this, the teacher resigned not long afterwards and moved to Australia to get away from Frane and his false sexual innuendos.

I was annoyed at this, as were many other kids, because she was a good teacher and didn't deserve that. But nobody said anything as Frane would only have punched them in the mouth. That's how Frane dealt with any criticism, no matter how trivial or justified that criticism was.

On a second occasion however, he had a run-in with Mr Hemmings, the headmaster. Hemmings was not only a signed-up member of the hang 'em and flog 'em brigade, but a complete sadist and he would discipline you for the slightest reason. In fact, he was such a sadist he caned more people in his first year than the previous headmaster, Mr Hesketh, had done in his 35 years at the school. But, he didn't just whack them with a stick but sliced their backsides so hard it was a wonder they didn't fly through the roof and out of the building. Frane should know because he got caned on several occasions and never kicked off about it. He knew the headmaster was justified in doing it even though he wasn't happy about it.

But then Frane's younger brother Billy got caught taking money from the younger kids, and the headmaster thought Frane had something to do with it. He hadn't. Hemmings wanted to cane Frane, but the latter told him that if he did, he would be caning him for something he hadn't done and he would never put up with that. Frane then grabbed Hemmings by the throat as though to emphasise the point and told him if he even thought of doing so he would find out where he lived and make life hell for him. Hemmings knew he wasn't joking, so he put his cane away and no more was said.

I left school in 1971 and I thought I would never see him again because I emigrated to Australia not long afterwards, along with the rest of my family. We were on one of those £10 schemes the government was offering people to persuade them to move out there at the time.

But one day, about thirty-five years later, I was watching television when Frane's face suddenly appeared on the screen.

I turned to my granddaughter and said, "I knew that guy... I went to school with him, and he was a real nasty piece of work."

Well he still was a nasty piece of work, because the news presenter said he was now a famous football hooligan involved in fights, stabbings, and mass brawls up and down the country. He was known as the Nightmare and I wasn't surprised about that because at school he had been a right bloody nightmare and I mean a right bloody nightmare.

So, as I say I was not surprised that the man was now a violent thug who used his fists to get his way, because that is exactly what he did at school, as anybody who was at school with him would tell you. Headmaster included.

BRIAN DEMINS

I was the one who introduced the Nightmare to football hooliganism and I still can't believe that was over forty years ago.

What happened was we were working at Cramwell's factory on the edge of Reading and somebody told him I was a member of the Berkshire Boot Boys, which was a group of hooligans who followed Reading football club up and down the country, but only to do battle with rival hooligans. He was instantly intrigued and asked how he could become a member of the firm. I told him to meet me in the Gates that Saturday, because that is where the firm always met up before a ruck ... and the rest as they say is history.

Frane turned up and immediately made his presence known. A lot of the lads knew him by reputation, or because they had gone to the same school as him, or lived on the same estate as he did, and knew he was amicable but not one to cross. But one person who didn't know him was David Rimmer. The latter was one of our older members and came from a different part of Reading to the Nightmare, which is why he did not know of Frane's fierce reputation and the consequences of getting on the wrong side of him.

    He soon did however, because after he had made it clear he did not like Frane and did not want him to be part of the firm, Frane headbutted him and sent him crashing to the ground with blood gushing out of his nose. He intended to follow through with a kick to the head for good measure, but before he could the Chester City 125s who were Reading's opponents that day, came crashing through the door and began laying into us left right and centre.

I know this story is in his autobiography *Nightmare* and so I am not going to go into detail about what happened next. I merely mention it to you to explain how the Nightmare got involved in football hooliganism and why he started rolling with the Berkshire Boot Boys

One story that does not appear in his autobiography however, was a ruck that we had with Aldershot's firm, the Aldershot A Company in February 1972. Now the reason I remember it well was because it was a cold winter's day and at that time Frane had been given the nickname the Nightmare because he was a bloody nightmare to contend with both on and off the pitch.

This particular incident came about after we had clocked the Aldershot firm coming towards us and we knew we had no chance of beating them because there were only eight of us and a hundred of them. In fact it was downright suicide making the trip to Aldershot in the first place, because most of our firm were down with the flu and there was no way we were going to beat a firm like Aldershot with such pitiful numbers.

The problem was though, that although the rest of the lads and me knew it, Frane did not. He seemed to think he was invincible and couldn't be beaten and at best that was stupid and at worst bloody idiotic.

In fact, it was bloody terrifying and as the Aldershot mob moved towards us menacingly, our first instinct was to turn and flee for our lives, but Frane said anybody who did that would have more things to worry about than the Aldershot mob because he would do them. So we all stayed where we were.

The Aldershot mob got closer and closer and then they started to charge at us clutching an assortment of weapons as they did. As I said, it was terrifying and was even more so because we knew that when they reached us we were going to get the biggest pasting in our lives.

But then a very strange thing happened, because as the Aldershot firm got nearer and saw that we weren't going to run, they began to slow a little, and then a bit more, and then a bit more until they came to a standstill about twenty yards away from us. They just stood looking at us with puzzled frowns on their faces.

I think they thought we were either mad or we were luring them into a trap and there were more of us lurking round the corner. So, they stood glaring at us scratching their heads in puzzlement until Frane, who had been standing there with an odd grin on his face, suddenly pulled out a gun and blasted it above their heads. This sent them fleeing for their lives and looking somewhat bug-eyed as they did.

They weren't the only ones. The rest of us were looking at him in astonishment too, because it was one thing turning up to engage in a punch-up but I drew the line at shooting people and so did the rest of the lads, well with one or two exceptions anyway.

I left the Berkshire Boot Boys after that, and set up a debt-collecting business to escape from football hooliganism because with the Nightmare running the firm, the only place I would wind up, was either the nut house or the prison. Of course I knew the Nightmare wouldn't be happy about it and might even kick up rough as some top boys did when people tried to leave their firm ... but he didn't. He just said that hooligans came and went all the time because that was the nature of football hooliganism and he wished me well in my new business, which surprised me a little but also pleased me with it.

   That said, I didn't escape the Nightmare completely because I would often see him around Reading and knew he was still involved in football violence because he loved telling me about it when we bumped into each other in the street or in a pub. Even if he hadn't told me about it I would still have known he was involved in football hooliganism, because his name would often appear in the local paper detailing his activities in one form or another over the next twenty years or so. That of course is when he wasn't in prison serving time for different offences.

But then, around 1996, Frane came to see me and asked me if I had any jobs at my debt-collecting agency, which by then was the biggest in Reading and the surrounding areas. I was surprised because I thought he made his money from drug dealing, or other criminal activities, but it seemed he was signing on the dole and the Department of Social Security had been putting pressure on him to find work.

 To be honest, I was in two minds about giving him a job because although my business was thriving and I did have vacancies, I wasn't sure he would make a good employee. I mean let's face it, the man was a violent thug whose only real talent was hitting people and putting the frighteners on them, and most employers are not looking for that in an employee. But, on the other hand the debt-collecting business is a funny game. People who are not afraid to put the frighteners on people are often the very people we are looking for, so I took him on with strict instructions that he wasn't to pull a gun out and shoot somebody if they did not pay up.

To be honest he was quite a good employee, because we only had to throw his name about and people tended to pay up. Well the ones who were dodgy themselves anyway as was the case with Harry Grimes.

Grimes owned a large garage on the edge of Reading and was refusing to pay an elderly painter and decorator for the work he had done for him, so the old man came to us. Now Grimes had already threatened the man using a couple of lads from his garage so I knew things could get heavy. However, when Grimes saw the Nightmare coming towards him he went as white as a ghost and he paid up immediately, particularly as the heavies that were with him backed off nervously before making themselves scarce.

The Nightmare did not work for me full time however. For one thing he never worked on a Saturday, his football hooligan activities took up his time on that day, and for another he was in and out of prison on a regular basis.

One thing I found strange however is that he never quit football hooliganism no matter how old he got. Most hooligans quit in their early twenties to start families or because of work, but he never did. He just continued on and on no matter how old and frail he became. He once told me that he would be a hooligan to the day he died. I didn't realise then he meant that literally. Incredible ... but there you go. A football hooligan to the day he dies, whenever that will be.

MICKEY CRANE

I first came across the Nightmare after I had a run in with his younger brother, Billy in the late seventies. At the time I was leader of the Chelsea Headhunters and Billy decided to take the piss out of me after we had come off second best against Sheffield United's firm, the Blades Service Crew.

Quite what made Billy have a dig at me I have no idea. I had never seen the man before and had no idea what he was doing in the pub. He certainly wasn't a member of our firm. I discovered later he was only there because he was supplying heroin to people in the pub, including members of my own firm. Still, I'm not going to say what happened next, as that is covered in my own autobiography as well as the Nightmare's, and you can read about it there.

What I will say is fists flew in all directions with me attacking members of his family, and Frane attacking members of mine. The feud only came to an end when a truce was agreed between him and me, which put an end to our little dispute once and for all.

I never liked the guy though, and wouldn't trust him as far as I could throw him, but the Nightmare never did anything to get my back up. This was possibly because he knew if he did I would give as good as I got, and possibly because he knew if he gave me hassle – or somehow managed to kill me, as he had threatened to do in the past – that would not save him. It wouldn't be long before someone came knocking on his front door with the intention of blowing his head off with a shotgun along with his brother Billy's for good measure.

I hated him if truth be told, and I went out of my way to avoid him, which wasn't easy because the man was an active member of the British Movement (BM) and often turned up at our rallies and when he did always greeted me like an old friend. Oh, I don't mean he was doing it to wind me up because he knew I hated his guts and he was trying to be funny ... I don't think the man had the mental capacity for that. I think he only saw what he wanted to see and nothing more.

A lot of former hooligans and indeed many of the current generation look upon the Nightmare as though he is some kind of Messiah figure. I don't know why. In my opinion his reputation is based on hype rather than anything else. Still, whenever I am approached by any football hooligan, whether or not they are still active in the hooligan game, the chances are they will ask me about my run-ins with him. To be honest it really pisses me off, because the man was just one of many hooligans I fought and he certainly wasn't the hardest or scariest. If you want my honest opinion he didn't even make it into the top ten scariest football hooligans of all time.

In my opinion, the real top ten scary hooligans are, and in no particular order, Harry the Dog (Millwall), Miss Barbara Whiplash (Ipswich), Chainsaw Charlie (Blackburn), Uriah
Thomas (Liverpool), Dani Lia (Wigan), Tommy the Baseball Bat Bush (QPR), Bobby the Wolf (West Ham), Paul Sykes (Leeds United), Hatchet Harry (Derby), and of course my own cousin Michaela Crane (Chelsea Headhunters).

I have, of course, left my own name off the list and the reason for this is not because it shouldn't be there because I think it should. The reason I have left it off is because I wouldn't want anybody to think I was egotistical, what with me being the nice modest guy I am.

    That said; I know some people are going to be astonished that the Nightmare is not included in my list and will only say he isn't because I don't like the man. Well I don't like Tommy the Baseball Bat Bush either or Paul Sykes for that matter, but they are there. My reason for not putting him on the list is not based on my dislike of the man, but because the Nightmare was not as scary, as these other hooligans were.

He didn't even come close to them. I mean he did not chop off the heads of rival hooligans and stick them on the gate of their home ground, as Chainsaw Charlie had done, and neither did he burn them alive at the crematorium where he worked as Uriah Thomas did. He didn't turn up at a rival hooligan's house with a shotgun and blast away as Harry the Dog had done, and Bobby the Wolf for that matter, or stick a red-hot poker up an opponent's backside and torture them as the notorious Miss Barbara Whiplash had done.

No, the Nightmare may be a legend in some people's eyes but he isn't a scary bastard ... well not compared to the likes of Miss Barbara Whiplash and Chainsaw Charlie anyway.

Still, anybody who knows anything about the Nightmare will tell you that he was heavily involved with the neo-Nazi terror group Combat 18 (C18) and he used the Chelsea Headhunters to recruit members for C18. I have no problem with that, because when I was top boy of the Headhunters, I used it to recruit members to the BM, which I was leading at the time. I had a problem with C18 however, and it was because it was a State asset. That is it was set up by MI5 to monitor the growing popularity of the far right in Britain and destroy it within.

Now I don't know if Frane was recruited before C18 was formed or after it was set up in 1992, but I will tell you this ... the man was an MI5 informer I have no doubt of that. This is because when C18 was formed, the main threat from the far right came from the British National Party (BNP), which at the time was surging in the polls and threatening to upset the established order. This was something that was reinforced when the BNP won a council seat in Tower Hamlets a couple of months later. So, MI5 got C18 to destroy the BNP from within by taking over the BNP Security Unit and carrying out racist attacks in its name. It hoped the BNP would get the blame, which it did, and that its popularity would plummet, which it did.

The reason I say I believed Frane was working for MI5 at this time, wasn't just because he often orchestrated these attacks, and carried them out along with other C18 goons, but because Frane was never convicted of any C18-related offences. This was despite the fact he was often photographed taking part in them by the Anti Nazi League (ANL) and other anti-fascist groups. Oh yes, I know it sounds crazy to claim that the State would allow its assets to engage in violent disorder and then stop them from getting prosecuted, but the State has a history of doing such things as any book on the security services will tell you.

What's more, football hooligans were perfect for spying on the far right because they tended to be young, white, and violent – the very people the far right attracted. They also tended to be susceptible to blackmail because once an undercover MI5 operative had secretly filmed them laying into rival hooligans with their fists and boots, as MI5 were fond of doing, they could blackmail them.

They could ask them to join the National Front (NF), or whichever far-right group they were interested in, and say to them tell us what they are up to or we will show the film to the police and you will go to jail. Now of course many did so because they were not only eager to stay out of jail, but also because MI5 paid them handsomely to do so. This is something which my cousin Michaela is very eager to tell you about. What's more, she will tell you why she also thinks Nightmare was a MI5 plant.

So without any further ado, over to you Michaela...

MICHAELA CRANE

Thanks Mickey...

Well, as my cousin said, I too believe the Nightmare was a State asset although I don't think he was recruited after C18 was formed in 1992, as Mickey thinks he may have been. I think he was recruited long before that, when he slashed a member of his own firm in the face for stabbing a sixty-year-old man with a knife and putting him in hospital. It was 1974 and he should have been jailed for it, but he wasn't. He wasn't even detained down at the police station for longer than an hour or two. He was just put in a cell for a brief period and then released without charge.

That was astonishing given the severity of his crime, but it was nothing new. The history of football hooliganism in Great Britain is one in which hooligans have often got away with their crimes in return for working on behalf of the State. By the State I mean MI5, the branch of the security services responsible for monitoring all extremist groups and making sure they do not destroy our democracy from within, as the Nazis had done in Germany when Hitler came to power in 1933.

The ways in which football hooligans were recruited by MI5 would often vary, but sometimes they went like this... A football hooligan is arrested for some offence or other and MI5 who already have them on their watch list because of their far-right connections are notified of their arrest and pay them a visit. They make them an offer and say to them... work for us and we will get the charges against you dropped, or if not we will see you go to jail for a long time and we mean a long time.

Now if you're wondering how MI5 has the authority to make such an offer, or indeed is in a position to pervert the course of justice to its own ends, then let me tell you. It's because the State grants them the power to do so. The State recognises that in order to pursue the interests of national security, it is often vital for MI5 to turn political extremists into State assets so they can spy on their colleagues and let them know what they are up to, instead of letting them go to jail for a crime they committed; no matter how violent that crime was.

To be honest I can understand that, because when somebody is a member of an extremist group they are often the best person to observe what the group is up to and whether they are planning any terrorist outrage. This would certainly explain why the charges against Frane were dropped and why he was never charged with the crime in relation to slashing a fellow hooligan across the face. At the time of the slashing, Frane was not only a member of the NF, but also the BM, and nobody was more violent than they were back in the seventies, not even the Ku Klux Klan over in the USA.

    That said; one question that needs to be asked is this ... If Frane was employed by the State to spy on fellow Nazis as far back as 1974, then why on earth did he spend so much time in prison for various hooligan-related offences over the years?

This is a good question and the answer lies in Frane's psychotic personality. Frane is a thug by nature and loves nothing more than beating people up and putting them in hospital. This is why he became a football hooligan in the first place and why he quickly became top boy of the Berkshire Boot Boys. The problem with people like Frane, however, is that it makes them virtually impossible to control, because they can't control their violent urges and so end up getting into a lot of scrapes. As such it means MI5 have a lot of difficulty keeping them out of prison; particularly as the more crimes they get away with, the more likely their neo-Nazi brethren will start asking questions and wondering whether they are spying on behalf of MI5.

This is why Frane has spent a lot of time in prison over the years for various hooligan-related offences, because if neo-Nazi groups had suspected he was spying on them he may well have ended up with a bullet in his head, as many who spy on those groups do.

Oh yes, I know people will say that I am only accusing the Nightmare of being a State asset because I don't like the man and am letting my feelings get the better of me, as they will do of Mickey, but what I tell you is the truth. The man is an utter bastard and I am not going to pretend otherwise, simply because people will get offended and call me all the names under the sun.

What's more, Frane used to spy on his far-right buddies inside prison too and pass on information about them to his MI5 handlers. In fact he spied on anybody MI5 was interested in. He would receive a lot of money for his services and once out of jail he was free to spend it on whatever he wished. In his case it was usually booze, women, and foreign holidays. Frane always went on holiday to Thailand or some other exotic destination after his release and although nobody ever asked him where he got the money from, it was from MI5; I have no doubt about that.

Perhaps the biggest help Frane was to MI5 however, came in 1993 when the BNP won a council seat at Tower Hamlets. Can you imagine that? Here are

MI5, tasked with monitoring groups like the BNP and ensuring they don't upset the natural order of things by winning elections, and there was the BNP winning an election and sticking two fingers up to the establishment in the process. I know the State was already worried about the growing popularity of the BNP by then, because a year earlier they had set up C18 to discredit the party from within, and I know Frane was central to their plans because he, more than anybody else, helped them do it.

Indeed, he did so by taking over the BNP's Security Unit along with the rest of his C18 goons and violently attacking their opponents with baseball bats, bottles, and knives. It was a clever move because once they had done so they could claim they were acting on behalf of the BNP and help MI5 destroy it from within as a consequence.

The BNP had won a council election by appearing moderate and throwing off their thuggish image, but the sight of C18 smashing baseball bats over people's heads and yelling Pakis out, soon put an end to that. By the time the next election came about, the BNP had lost public support and the election with it.

Another thing about Frane is that the State also used him to spy on the loyalist paramilitaries. The British far right have always had links to terrorist groups like the Ulster Defence Association (UDA) and Ulster Freedom Fighters (UFF) and MI5 were only too keen to play on such links to create havoc amongst loyalist terror groups and destroy them internally as they had done with far-right groups such as the National Socialist Movement.

If I am honest I can understand this too, because at the time the loyalist paramilitaries were committing far more murders than the Irish Republican Army (IRA) were, and that is saying something. What's more, there were rumours the loyalists were eager to kill targets on mainland Britain in order to prevent the government signing the Good Friday Agreement which it was planning on doing.

Therefore, in order to prevent further bloodshed, Frane, and other MI5 spies were ordered to use their far-right links to spy on them and destroy any terrorist plot in the process.

Now I don't know how successful Frane was in doing so, but I will tell you this. I know of at least two occasions where the loyalist paramilitaries were thwarted in their plans to spread terror on the streets of London, after somebody on the far right had grassed them up to MI5 handlers.

The first occasion was when a well-known loyalist was stopped at Belfast harbour, and his car searched after the police were tipped off that he was on his way to London to kill members of the annual troops' movement, which many saw as an IRA front. The tip off was proved correct when a gun was subsequently found hidden in a secret compartment of his boot. And the second was when MI5 were tipped off that the UDA were planning on assassinating Ken Livingston, the former leader of the Greater London Council for his alleged support of the IRA.

Turning to Frane's anti Paki bashing activities however, I think it was in 1979 that I first started hearing the name Andi Ali banded about at neo-Nazi events up and down the country. The word was that he was a very hard bastard and had knocked out a couple of the NF skinheads who had turned up in Blackburn hoping to engage in a spot of Paki bashing. I was so enraged when I heard this that I was determined to go to Blackburn and break his legs, as indeed was Mickey, and other Nazi skinheads I knew.

However, nothing came of it because Joey Porter, who was the number one crime boss in London at the time, did not want gang warfare on his hands. So, I left it at that.

But then in 2004, I started hearing rumours that the Nightmare was gunning for Andi Ali after the latter had been named as the number-one target on a BNP hit list called Redwatch. Over the years I have come across a lot of Pakis who can handle themselves in a fight such as Riaz Khan who was leader of Leicester City's hooligan firm the Baby Squad, or Bazzar Khan who was said to be the hardest Asian in Birmingham. But none of them could handle themselves as well as Ali could. If you were to draw up a list of the ten hardest Pakis of all time, then Ali would be top of it, no doubt about it.

When Ali was named as the number-one target, it was because he was conducting academic research on the BNP, and its links to C18. Now this really pissed off the Nightmare and everybody else on the far right with it, because with Ali being such a target of Redwatch, you would have thought he would have laid low for a while wouldn't you through fear of getting a bullet in his head but he didn't. Far from it. Instead, he used to turn up at BNP demonstrations and walk up to them and their C18 buddies and say, *"Well, boys I'm here ... what are you going to do about it? Wave your fists and try to look scary. Oh I am scared."* He even did so to Frane on a number of occasions, which is one of the reasons Ali has become a legend in anti-fascist circles and a figure of hate on the far right. The funny thing about Andi Ali though, is that he was never a criminal, but a law-abiding citizen who never broke the law and never ever served time in prison.

Still, the Nightmare never took a swing at Ali whenever the latter confronted him, despite saying he was gunning for him and wanted him dead. It is this and all the other reasons listed here that puzzle me as to how Frane has achieved cult status amongst far-right activists and football hooligans alike. He was nowhere near as hard as they say he was; or as scary. Indeed, I would describe him as nothing more than a vicious little bully who has acquired legendary status because others believe the hype he has written about himself in his book *Nightmare...* and nothing more.

Recently, I heard that the Nightmare attended an English Defence League (EDL) march where he accidently ran into Tommy the Baseball Bat Bush who he had been bad-mouthing since the seventies. That ended with Tommy headbutting him and Frane winding up splat out on the floor covered in blood.

As I said, his fierce reputation is built on hype and nothing but hype. Trust me!

KARL CRISPEN

I first met the Nightmare when he came into my local boozer to drink and enjoy a powwow with the rest of the lads. It was 1996, I had just turned seventeen, and I had joined the Berkshire Boot Boys to become a football hooligan and have it out with other football hooligans.

To be honest, I didn't have a clue who he was when I first saw him because he was running with the Chelsea Headhunters and spent most of his time in London chilling out with the Chelsea mob. When I was told he was the infamous Nightmare I was in awe, because I had been hearing about his exploits for years and in my eyes the man was a fucking legend.

Fighting wise, the man was a right lunatic and would always lead the Berkshire Boot Boys into battle whenever Reading were playing at home and he could not be bothered to go down to London to help the Chelsea Headhunters do battle with whoever they were up against that day. I would often be behind him and he clearly had no fear of anybody or anyone. He would simply jump into the opposition and begin lashing out with his fists, boots, head, or whatever. Indeed, I lost count of the number of times I saw him headbutt one hooligan after another.

To be honest, the man should have been certified insane, because he certainly wasn't the full shilling. In fact, it always amazed me how he managed to avoid the nuthouse, because he was certainly just as crazy as all the other hooligans who were sent there, such as Hatchet Harry and Tommy the Baseball Bat.

From the age of sixteen, the Nightmare had been attending far-right demonstrations and campaigning against non-white immigration in Britain. He often used to rant about blacks and other non-whites and how they were pouring into the country despite there being no black in the Union Jack. On more than one occasion I saw him storm up to a black person in a pub, or out on the street, and punch them in the face simply because the colour of their skin was not white.

The Nightmare was particularly scathing of Pakis and it bordered on the obsessive. I knew he had been a member of the BM in his youth, and that he rated them more than the NF, because they were forever going into Paki areas and engaging in Paki bashing, which the NF did not do as much. Still, the thing about football hooliganism is that he found it hard to engage in Paki bashing because Pakis rarely got involved in football hooliganism. Well not back in the seventies anyway.

He once told me that Reading had got Bradford away in early 1978, and he had been really looking forward to that one because he could not resist the opportunity of fighting the Pakis on their own turf ... and the town was full of them. However, when he got there he was staggered to discover that Bradford's firm the Ointment didn't have a Paki amongst them. When he asked them why, he was told the Pakis kept themselves to themselves, and did not bother them, so they didn't bother the Pakis.

Well the Nightmare was so enraged that he wanted to go into the Paki area and have it out with them, but the Bradford firm had other ideas. They pointed out that the Reading firm were on their turf and if Frane and his mates did not piss off back to Reading straight away, they would do them. This of course made Frane see red and fists flew in all directions. It didn't do the Nightmare much good though, because with the Bradford mob fighting on their own turf they had the men and muscle to deal with it, and it wasn't long before the Reading mob were heading back home with their tails between their legs, and their egos bruised.

A funny thing about the Nightmare, however, was that when we lost a fight and it wasn't anybody's fault, he would never kick off about it and punch somebody in the face saying it was their fault when he knew it wasn't, as some top boys did. He would simply shrug it off and say, "Some you win and some you lose," before adding with a smile, "besides we'll get the bastards back the next time our sides meet."

That said if somebody did cause us to lose a fight because of cowardice or their stupidity, he really did have a go at them as Billy Higgins discovered to his cost in March 1998.

Billy was a year or two older than I was and a bit of a ladies' man and he never missed the opportunity to chat up a good-looking bird when the opportunity arose. Now this wasn't a problem most of the time, because we were all young and always chatting up girls ourselves, but on this particular day we were fighting Southend's firm the CS Crew and Frane told him to go outside and keep an eye out for them, so they didn't storm the pub and take us by surprise.

Well that's exactly what the CS Crew did ... knocking us for six in the process. The only reason they had managed to take us by surprise was because Billy had vacated his post and gone chasing after some bird he had spotted walking past the pub in a short skirt a little while earlier.

Well the Nightmare was fuming as you can imagine and went hunting for Billy. He found him a couple of streets away sitting on a park bench with the bird in tow, so he grabbed him by the neck and beat him so hard that Billy was in intensive care for a month feeding from a hospital drip, and rueing the day he had decided to vacate his post.

   Another hooligan who incurred his wrath for not taking his hooligan activities seriously was David Henshaw. Now to be honest, the man was more of a liability than anything else, because he was a druggie and an alcoholic and when he wasn't pissed he was usually as high as a kite on heroin or some other banned substance. In fact he was a walking wreck and certainly couldn't be relied upon to put up a good fight whenever we got into a ruck.

   This was certainly the case when we came up against Leicester City's Baby

Squad in 1999. We were playing them away and Frane was really looking forward to this one because this was the one firm in the country whose top boy was a Paki and Frane hated Pakis as I said before. He warned everybody to be bright and alert for the fight and everybody obeyed and turned up sober except for Henshaw. He was half pissed when he boarded the coach, so Frane beat him to a pulp before throwing him off the coach and over a hedge where he landed face first in a pile of cow shit. If you took the time to get to know the Nightmare then you would discover he wasn't as bad as people made out that he was. He never took the piss out of anybody who was disabled or had learning disabilities, as some hooligans did, because he didn't think it was right to attack those who were physically disabled and vulnerable and couldn't fight back.

Now to be honest I found that quite surprising given the man was a Nazi and the Nazis had euthanised many disabled people because they considered them of no importance to humanity whatsoever. I was even more surprised when on one occasion we were having a drink in the Grapes and some builders walked in pushing a disabled man through the door as they did.

Now it was clear they didn't know the disabled man from Adam, because one of them said to him, "I don't know who you are but if you don't buy us our dinner, I'm going to put you in hospital for a month, and on a drip at that."

Well the disabled man was so terrified he began fumbling in his pocket for his wallet, but the Nightmare just went over and told the bozos to piss off and leave the man alone or else.

Well I thought the bozos were going to have a fit and the one who had threatened the disabled man moved forward menacingly. Frane headbutted him, sending him tumbling to the ground and then he began jumping on his head for good measure.

As I said earlier, I like the Nightmare and rate him as the hardest hooligan ever, but even he could bite off more than he could chew at times. I knew he was an ardent supporter of the loyalist cause in Northern Ireland because he was always turning up at St Patrick Day parades and yelling abuse at the Fenians and calling them all the names under the sun. I knew it really got under his skin to see so many Irish celebrating their heritage. He thought most of them were IRA supporters even when they weren't, especially if they were waving green flags and not Union Jacks as the hordes of loyalist protesters behind him were.

Quite often, the Nightmare would confront people if he heard them speaking with an Irish accent and ask if they were Catholic before punching them in the face and accusing them of being IRA supporters if they said yes. He would also grab their wallets and take down their addresses to ensure they didn't go running to the police. Most of the time Frane experienced no repercussions because of this, but Sean Mcfallon was different. He was a seventeen-year-old spotty faced lad from London who was studying history at Reading University, and although Frane hadn't expected any hassle to come his way after he had heard him speaking with an Irish accent and broken his jaw in the process, it certainly did come his way and big time too.

This was because the lad was the nephew of Semus Mcfallon and the latter was not only the head of the notorious

Mcfallon crime family but was also somebody who ran most of North London on terror. So, the Nightmare very wisely decided to go into hiding and wound up lying low at a friend's house in Liverpool hoping the whole thing would blow over and he could return to Reading when it had.

But then he went and got himself into a pub fight and wound up getting stabbed in the leg in the process. That was bad enough, but the story made the national papers and it wasn't long before the Mcfallon family got to hear of it and sent heavies up to Liverpool to deal with Frane and teach him a lesson he would not forget.

Now I know the Nightmare got his legs broken and wound up in intensive care for a couple of months, but why they didn't just put a bullet in his head, and send him back home to Reading in a coffin was a mystery to me. That's normally what happened to people who crossed the Mcfallon family, whether they had intended to or not.

Another person the Nightmare regretted taking on was Celtic's top boy, Rory McNeal. The Nightmare really hated him with a passion and I mean with a passion. The rivalry between Celtic and Rangers was infamous, but that was nothing compared to the rivalry between Frane and McNeal. These two couldn't stand the sight of each other and why the Nightmare never mentioned that in his autobiography, I don't know but he didn't.

Years later I remember him telling me that the reason why he and McNeal never got on was because the Celtic Soccer Crew, were a bunch of Fenian bastards who supported the IRA, and had actually provided weapons and a safe house for one of their top men when he came over to kill some UDA man who was living in Aberdeenshire. Indeed, the latter was not only blasted to death on his front door, but neither McNeal, nor his terrorist friends were ever charged with murder because the police did not have enough evidence to do so.

I remember saying to Frane, "Well surely the UDA sent somebody over to kill him and the rest of the Celtic crew, or they got one of the Rangers firm to do it, because they had strong links to the UDA?"

But Frane just said, "No." He said they should have done and wanted to, but they didn't, because the UDA was heavily involved in the drug trade in Glasgow at the time, as indeed were the IRA. Neither side wanted a turf war in Glasgow as that would affect the huge sums both were making from the drugs' trade. So the UDA told the Nightmare to lay off McNeal and the IRA did the same with the latter.

However, the Nightmare stupidly ignored it and confronted McNeal outside a pub getting into a fight with him and leaving both of them battered and bruised. He has done some bloody stupid things in his time and put himself in great danger, but none were as silly as this. The UDA were a terrorist organisation and were clearly not people to piss about with. So, they lured Frane to an out-of-the way spot near Glasgow where he was shot in the kneecaps and told never to defy UDA orders again, or next time they would put a bullet in his head.

I stopped being a football hooligan in 2002 and went to work for a mate of mine in Spain who had just opened a bar. The Nightmare said he would come over and see me but he never has. The fact of the matter is if you weren't with him on Saturdays kicking the hell out of fellow hooligans, then he soon forgot who you were and you would never see him again, well not if you lived out in Spain anyway.

Still, I now have a bar of my own on the Costa Brava and many of my punters are current or former football hooligans who ran with one firm, or another. When I tell them that I was a member of the Berkshire Boot Boys back in the nineties, the very first thing they ask me is about the Nightmare and what sort of man he is.

"A fucking lunatic…" I always reply, "…a lunatic and nothing but a lunatic."

HARRY the DOG

I was top dog of Millwall's firm, the notorious F-Troop back in the seventies, and I never met the Nightmare, because our teams never clashed on match day. I was aware of his existence however, because when you're top dog of a hooligan firm you tend to know who all the other top boys are, particularly if they have such a violent reputation as the Nightmare had.

One of the stories I heard about him regarded a clash he had with Mansfield's firm, The Shady Express, back in the seventies. It must have been around 1977 because I seem to recall it was the same year as the Silver Jubilee, but I cannot remember the exact date because I never kept a diary on these things.

Anyway, what happened is that both clubs were playing away and by chance both firms pulled into the same service station to get some grub and stretch their legs as football hooligans do when they are on their way to a football ruck. The first the Nightmare knew about it however, was when he noticed a large group of lads lurking about near their coach and drinking beer and chatting amongst themselves. Even though he didn't know what firm they belonged to, he knew instinctively that they were football hooligans. When you've been a hooligan for a while, you tend to recognise other football hooligans when you see them, even if your paths have never crossed before.

So, the Nightmare quickly went over and asked who they were. After being told they were members of The Shady Express, he headbutted the nearest one to him sending him crashing to the floor with blood pouring out of his mouth and his mates looking on in horror.

Now some people might consider that was bad form because in the hooligan world there is an unspoken rule which states that you must never attack a rival firm if you come across them at a service station or anywhere else unless you are expecting to fight them on that day. If you do attack them it means you are stopping them fighting whoever it is they are expecting to fight and in the hooligan world that should never happen. It does of course happen, partly because hooligans sometimes mistake other firms for their rivals, and partly because many of them just don't care, and want a good scrap anyway.

The Nightmare of course did want a good scrap on that occasion, and it led to fists flying in all directions as both firms tore into each other with a frenzy that was apparently painful to watch.

Throughout the late seventies, I used to hear his name being bandied about at Anti Nazi League (ANL) demonstrations that I attended. Although he would often turn up at ANL rallies with his neo-Nazi mates and they would lay into the ANL with their fists and boots, he never did so when I was around. This was even though he knew I was active within the ANL and would possibly be at one of their protests. In fact if you want my honest opinion the man deliberately avoided me because he knew if we had met I would have put him in hospital along with the rest of his Nazi goons.

The most disgusting attack the Nightmare ever carried out though, at least on a ANL protestor, was when he smashed a placard over the head of a seventy-seven- year-old ANL demonstrator called Gladys Crompton after he saw her waving her placard and yelling, *"Black and white unite"* on the other side of her road.

He left her flat out on the pavement. Now given Gladys' age it was a wonder he didn't kill her and I was so angry I shot up to Reading and went looking for the bastard hoping to smash the ANL placard over his head. I couldn't find him, but I did spot one of his neo-Nazi mates coming out of his local boozer so I smashed it down on his head instead. I told him to tell the Nightmare it was Harry the Dog who had done it and God help him when I find him.

I never did find the bastard though. This was because shortly afterwards, I was forced to flee to Australia after a well-known gangster had put out a contract on me, after somebody blasted Mickey Crane with a shotgun and the word on the street was that it was me. It wasn't, but if I had found Frane I would have put him in intensive care that's for sure.

From what I knew about the Nightmare I believed he wanted to be top boy but he knew that he wasn't as hard as I was ... or some of the other top boys around at the time, such as Dani Lia and Tommy the Baseball Bat Bush. Bush had recently headbutted the Nightmare and left him unconscious on a pavement, after they had met by chance at an EDL demonstration outside Hyde Park. This was despite both of them approaching middle age.

I also knew he feared Mickey Crane because the latter was a real hard bastard and would have beaten the Nightmare in a one-to-one fight, which is why he never tried to become the Chelsea Headhunters' top boy when Crane held that role and why he never went anywhere near Chelsea.

I know this may seem strange given I have never met him but I don't have a good thing to say about the Nightmare. I have never seen any good points in him at all. Today, many former hooligans look upon him with cult status but I don't know why because he certainly doesn't deserve it or is anywhere near as terrifying as they make out. Of course the Nightmare may take offence at what I have said about him and belittle me for it. But one thing is for sure, he will not fight me over it. He wouldn't back in the seventies and he won't now. That's the type of man he is.

Bloody coward!

BILLY FRANE

I have read what Harry the Dog has said about my brother, the infamous Nightmare, and I have to laugh. My brother has never been frightened of him or anybody else for that matter and the only reason they never clashed at an ANL protest was because Harry never turned up when he was there.

That wasn't my brother's fault because he didn't know if Harry would be there or not, he did not even know the man, because Reading and Millwall never met on match day, well not in the late seventies anyway when Harry was actively involved with the hooligan scene. So, for Harry to claim that my brother deliberately avoided turning up at ANL demonstrations because he was frightened of him and was terrified Harry would do him over if he did is laughable at best, and ludicrous at worst.

What is even more ludicrous is the idea that my brother deliberately smashed a placard over the head of a seventy-seven-year-old woman ... because he did not. It's true he did strike her over the head with it but that was by accident rather than by design. What happened was the ANL were holding a demonstration in East London to protest at the growing number of assaults on non-white citizens by the NF and other far-right groups, and my brother went along to show his support for the NF and hopefully to kick the fuck out of the ANL in the process.

When he saw the ANL waving their yellow and black placards in the air and shouting black and white unite, he saw red and went storming over, somehow managing to avoid the rows of police officers who were standing guard between both groups and maintaining law and order in the process.

Once he got to the ANL he grabbed the placard from the old woman because she just happened to be the nearest one to him, and went to smash it down on the ANL bozo next to her – a spotty face college student who had been yelling abuse at him across the road. However, the old dear got in the way and unfortunately she ended up getting hit instead. It was an accident, as I said before, because there is no way on earth that my brother would deliberately strike someone who was elderly; as Karl Crispen will tell you.

Karl has already told you that my brother would never hit a disabled person because he does not think it right to attack somebody who is physically incapable of defending themselves and the same goes for elderly people too. My brother has never hit an elderly person in his life, well apart from that old dear which was an accident. He would not hit somebody who was old and frail and who could not put up much resistance, as Dereck Horbins would confirm.

Horbins was a member of our firm in the early seventies and made the mistake of hitting a sixty-year-old man in the face after we had taken over a pub in Aldershot to await the arrival of the Aldershot A Company who we were up against that day. Well the locals went berserk and confronted Horbins. He looked at my brother thinking he was going to come to his rescue, but the Nightmare never did.

Indeed, he was so incensed by what Horbins had done he just said, "Fuck him" and left the pub with Teddy Mitsker and the rest of the lads and leaving Horbins to his fate.

Still, it is true that Harry the Dog went storming up to Reading to confront my brother about it but could not find him and ended up smashing an ANL placard down on one of his neo-Nazi mates instead, but it wasn't my brother's fault he couldn't find him. He did not know he was coming. If he had he would have been waiting for him and had it out with him in a one-to-one fight.

    As soon as the Nightmare found out about what Harry had done, he went storming down to Harry's local boozer intending to smash a NF placard down on his head. However, he wasn't there so he smashed it down on one of his hooligan mates instead and told him to tell Harry it was the Nightmare who had done it and if he had a problem with it, then he knew where to find him.

    I don't know what would have happened if my brother and Harry had ever met, but the fight never took place because Harry was forced to flee to Australia after being wrongly accused of attempting to kill Mickey Crane. But I will tell you this; my brother would not have backed away from a fight with Harry the Dog. He wouldn't then and wouldn't now. That is the type of man he is.

So bring it on Harry, if you dare.

It's also laughable what that poofter Mickey Crane has said about my brother, because as with everything Crane says, it's all bullshit and is so far detached from reality it defies belief.

It is true that Crane headbutted me and left me splat out in a pool of blood, after I had taken the piss out of him for getting done over by the Sheffield Blades Crew along with the rest of his Chelsea firm. However, the only reason my brother agreed to a truce with him was because Crane threatened my daughter. When my brother heard that he had assaulted me and left me with a broken nose, he was so angry about it he shot down to his local boozer hoping to put Crane in hospital, but because he wasn't there he ended up stabbing an off-duty police officer instead,

 Crane was terrified when he heard that because he knew that my brother would be gunning for him once he got out of prison and might even kill him, so in desperation he threatened my daughter. At the time my daughter was only nine years old and Crane sent me a picture of her standing outside her school along with the words, *Mess with me, and your little girl is going to get hurt, got it!*

So that's why my brother never went after Crane once he got out of prison. It's also why Crane is still alive today to write his autobiography, which he recently has done, along with that cousin of his who has recently published her autobiography; *Michaela Crane: The shocking story of Britain's hardest football hooligan, and the Chelsea Headhunters' top girl.*

One football hooligan whom the Nightmare really got on with though, was the infamous Hatchet Harry.

Back in the seventies, he was known as Derby County's top boy before he went and chopped off the heads of rival hooligans, was certified insane, and was sent to Broadmoor for the rest of his life.

My brother never met Hatchet Harry when he was a hooligan because their teams never met on match day as Harry himself says in his book, *Hatchet Harry, Football Hooligan and Derby Lunatic Fringe (DLF) Thug*, but he nonetheless admired the man and often went to visit him in Broadmoor until the latter's tragic death from cancer in the summer of 2021.

Now some people may find it odd they never met until my brother visited Harry in Broadmoor, given they were also members of the NF in the seventies and regularly attended NF demonstrations around the country but they didn't. I don't know why that was but my brother often used to talk about far-right politics with him and Harry loved it. It reminded him of the good old days, and the times he used to go out Paki bashing and putting them in hospital along with other unwashed scum.

One story my brother told me about Hatchet Harry concerned a Paki family who had moved onto his estate and took over a corner shop, which had previously been owned by a white couple he knew well. Harry was fuming when he heard that and went round and told the Paki owner to piss off and get the hell out of his estate, because this was a Paki free zone. Well the man and his family did move away, but only after Harry had burned down their shop, along with their car for good measure.

A second story my brother told me about Harry involved a Paki who had moved to Reading and got a job as a taxi driver. This made Harry see red particularly when he saw him pull up on his estate to let an old woman out of his car. Indeed, Harry was so incensed when he saw him, that he went over and put a hatchet to the man's neck – he always carried it with him and it was how he got the name Hatchet Harry in the first place – and told him that if he ever saw him on his estate again he would hack off his head and stick it on a pole for all to see.

Well the Paki was so terrified he fled back to Pakistan and was never heard of again. This was probably a good thing because as we now know, when Harry threatened to chop his head off he wasn't kidding, because that is precisely what he was doing to football hooligans up and down the country ... although nobody knew it at the time.

A second hooligan my brother really got on with was the notorious Paul Sykes, which is surprising really given Sykesy was not a racist and never shared my brother's racist views. Indeed, my brother never understood why Sykesy did not share his hatred of Pakis given he was from Wakefield and the place was overrun by them, but he didn't and as I said it puzzled him.

    My brother didn't meet Sykes when he was a hooligan because he was a lot older than he was and he ran the Leeds United Service Crew firm when my brother was still at school. But, he rated him as the hardest hooligan that ever lived, certainly harder than Dani Lia, who was said to be the hardest hooligan in the seventies, and ran with Wigan

Athletic's firm, the appropriately named Goon Squad.

The reason he rated him highly as a fighter however, was because he served time with him in prison and knew what a formidable fighter he was. Now I know from my own time in jail that all prisons have their hard men and all the hard men were feared, but nobody was as feared as Paul Sykes was. Indeed, in the seventies he was known as the hardest prisoner in Britain and with good reason.

On one occasion my brother saw Sykes go into some Paddy's cell and knock the bastard out with one punch for playing his music too loud, and refusing to turn it down, despite the fact the man was over seven feet tall and a bare-knuckle fighter champion with it. While on another occasion he knocked out the infamous Lee Duffy in a one-on-one fight despite Duffy being the hardest man in

Middlesbrough and twenty years his junior.

Still I'm not going to tell you anything more about Sykes' hooligan days, and the fights he got into during those days, because you can read all about it in his autobiography *Hooligan Agony: Anecdotes on Wakefield's Paul Sykes. Football Hooligan, and the Leeds United Service Crew's Top Boy*. All I will say it is a good read and I mean a damn good read.

The hooligan who my brother really hated more than anyone else, was Tommy the Baseball Bat Bush and with good reason. The man was a vile rapist and when he wasn't leading the Queen Park Rangers Bushbabies into action, he was raping women and killing them with it.

Indeed, on one occasion he even raped a woman police officer who was guarding him while he was in hospital recovering from an injury he sustained after a botched robbery attempt. Now if you don't believe me then read his autobiography, *Tommy the Baseball Bat, Queen Park Rangers (QPR) hooligan and English Defence League (EDL) thug*, and see for yourself because he boasts about it in that book.

My brother never actually met Bush during his time as a hooligan, because, as with Harry the Dog, their teams never met on match days. However, he wished they had met because my brother hates rapists even more than he hates Pakis and all the other unwashed scum. In fact, if they had met back in the seventies when Bush was active on the hooligan scene I have no doubt my brother would have put him in hospital despite Bush being a hard bastard with a psychopathic reputation for violence that rivalled his own. This is because my brother hates people who abuse women just as he hates those who abuse the disabled and elderly.

That said; my brother did actually bump into Bush forty years later when he was attending an EDL protest in London and yelling abuse at the Unite Against Fascism (UAF) in the process. What happened was my brother was just watching the UAF heckling the EDL and yelling, *"Nazi scum of our streets!",* when a well-known Paki called Bazzar Khan began tearing into the EDL knocking a few of them out in the process.

My brother could hardly take his eyes off Khan as he had never seen the man before but knew of him and knew that he was a violent nutter with a reputation for psychotic violence that matched his own. Indeed Khan had recently been touted as the new Andi Ali, the hardest Paki that ever lived.

But then my brother noticed an elderly man next to him and yelled, "Fuck me it's Tommy the Baseball Bat Bush isn't it?"

Now Bush was taken aback by this because he had never met my brother in his life and he said, "Who the fuck are you?"

My brother said he was the Nightmare, and he had led the Berkshire Boot Boys back in the seventies.

Bush saw red and yelled, "You're the prat who appeared in that BBC documentary aren't you ... a few years back ... saying you would like to castrate me?" He then headbutted my brother leaving him flat out on the floor in a pile of blood.

Now my brother was fuming when he came to, and wanted to knock Bush out and put him in hospital for a month, but he never got the chance. Bush was already down at the local police station having his fingerprints taken because of the assault.

In fact, he was also having his DNA taken too because Bush had lived in Florida since the eighties, and it wasn't on the DNA database.

The results from the database took everybody by surprise, because his DNA linked him to an unsolved murder case going back to the seventies ... the murder of a civil servant called Alison Jones to be precise. Bush had raped and killed her, simply because she had offended him by putting pressure on him to find a job in the dole office she worked at when he went to sign on one day.

That was unbelievably petty as was the fact that Bush had headbutted my brother because he had appeared in a BBC documentary belittling him. My brother never asked to be in that documentary and was only in it because he was secretly filmed by an undercover journalist discussing his hooligan days.

Bush is locked up in prison these days in a sex offenders' unit where my brother can't get to him and put him in hospital where he deserves. Still he has every intention of doing so when he comes out of prison, because my brother never forgets an insult and always pays a debt.

So Mr Bush if you don't already know it, you are a marked man. You should be worried, very worried, because when the Nightmare comes looking for you, hell usually follows. And I do mean hell, as football hooligans up and down the country will tell you, Mickey Crane included.

FINAL WORD FROM THE AUTHOR

So, you've read the stories of Britain's most prolific hooligan from those who knew him, or in the case of Harry the Dog knew of him, and I leave it to you to decide if the man deserves the godlike status he is considered to hold by some sections of the football hooligan community, both past and present.

Has your opinion of the Nightmare changed since reading this book, and if so how?

I believe the man is a violent psychopath who was attracted to football hooliganism because of the violence that came with it and the opportunities it afforded him to indulge in his violent tendencies. Is it surprising therefore that a man like this would still be engaging in football hooliganism at a time when all the other hooligans of his generation had long since given up fighting their rivals on terraces, backstreets, and pubs up and down the country.

My view of the Nightmare hasn't changed since the first book I wrote about him. I thought then he was a violent psychopath and not one to cross, and I still believe that now, no matter how much Mickey Crane and Harry the Dog have tried to convince me otherwise, and make out that his reputation is based on nothing more than hype.

One of the things I find most astonishing when it comes to the Nightmare however, is how he has managed to survive all these years without somebody putting a bullet in his head, given the calibre of people he has upset along the way. They include people such as Rory McNeal and gangland boss Semus

Mcfallon, not to mention terrorist groups like the UDA and IRA.

We've heard from Mickey Crane, that he believed the Nightmare was a State asset who was protected by MI5 and was able to live the life he did knowing the State would protect him from people and keep him from harm, but there is absolutely no evidence to support that. Indeed, all the evidence suggests that the State did not like the Nightmare and never missed an opportunity to jail him. This is why he has spent so many years in prison and has received bigger sentences than most football hooligans have done, Mickey Crane included and his notorious cousin Michaela ... perhaps the real MI5 assets...

A second thing I find astonishing about the Nightmare however, is how reluctant he has been to talk about his violent past and write an autobiography on his hooligan days, when so many of his contemporaries have urged him to do so such as Teddy Mitsker and Karl Crispen. This is even more astonishing given that many hooligans like nothing more than to boast about their football exploits, both on talk shows, and on YouTube and other social media outlets. They like to say how hard they were and what naughty boys they were when they ran one firm or other. This is further evidence that the Nightmare is not bothered about the fame football hooliganism has brought him and he was simply in it for the violence.

Finally, Billy Frane has told you that the Nightmare was recently assaulted at an EDL march after Tommy the Baseball Bat Bush, headbutted him and left him in a pool of blood for comments he made about Tommy when he was being secretly filmed by an undercover journalist in June 2007. This is true; he was, but only because he hit the Nightmare out of the blue and took him by surprise. He didn't give him time to defend himself and fight back because he knew if he had, then the Nightmare would have knocked him out and put him in hospital.

So once again, I don't believe the rumours that Michaela Crane has recently been spreading that the Nightmare's reputation is based on hype and nothing more than hype because it isn't.

His reputation is based on the fact he is a violent nutter; who loves nothing more than a good fight, and isn't afraid of getting stuck into rival firms and leading from the front as all top boys should. Something that hooligans past and present would admit, Mickey Crane included.

The Nightmare Calling

Printed in Great Britain
by Amazon